Phyllis Wong and the Forgotten Secrets of Mr Okyto

Geoffrey McSKIMMING

From the bestselling author of the CAIRO JIM CHRONICLES

ALLEN&UNWIN
SYDNEY • MELBOURNE • AUCKLAND • LONDON

First published in 2012

Allen & Unwin
83 Alexander Street
Crows Nest NSW 2065
Australia
Phone: (61 2) 8425 0100
Fax: (61 2) 9906 2218
Email: info@allenandunwin.com
Web: www.allenandunwin.com

A Cataloguing-in-Publication entry is available from the National Library of Australia
www.trove.nla.gov.au

ISBN 978 1 74237 821 3

Cover and text design by Seymour Designs
Cover and internal illustrations by Peter Sheehan
Author photograph by Sue-Anne Webster (picture frame: iStockphoto)
Set in 12/17 pt Sabon by Midland Typesetters, Australia
This book was printed in June 2012 at McPherson's Printing Group, 76 Nelson St, Maryborough, Victoria 3465, Australia.
www.mcphersonsprinting.com.au

10 9 8 7 6 5 4 3 2 1

The paper in this book is FSC® certified. FSC® promotes environmentally responsible, socially beneficial and economically viable management of the world's forests.

Phyllis Wong and the FORGOTTEN SECRETS of MR OKYTO

For Sue-Anne Webster

PART ONE

PART TWO

PART THREE

PART ONE

The mystery of the blue wren bookends

Distress for Mrs Lowerblast

Phyllis Wong's unravelling of all the secrets began on the first afternoon of her end-of-term vacation.

The last few months of school hadn't been especially hard or bothersome. She had done well in most of her subjects, and had even come first in History. And she had, over the course of the term, learnt and practised and added another six conjuring tricks—four card routines, one coin transposition and, the classic of them all, the cups and balls—to her growing repertoire of magic.

The joy and thrill of performing magic ran through Phyllis Wong's veins. Her father said she had inherited it from her great-grandfather, Wallace Wong, Conjuror of Wonder! Before his mysterious disappearance in Venezuela while performing the Houdini sub-trunk illusion in 1936, Wallace Wong had been one of the most famous and highest-paid magicians in the world.

Wherever the passion had come from, Phyllis loved magic. She had loved magic from as far back as she could remember. She loved the elegance of a good trick; the way it mesmerised her audience and transported them away from their worlds and their thoughts and their worries for a few moments. And she loved the small, surging thrill she always had when the moment of the vanish or the substitution or the re-appearance or the totally unexpected *manifestation* of an object happened.

That always made her zing.

When she performed her magic, Phyllis Wong knew how the mysteries worked. But she was soon to find out that there were *other* mysteries floating about in the world that were *not* so straightforward.

'Hi, Mrs L.,' Phyllis called as she and her miniature fox terrier, Daisy, entered Lowerblast's Antiques & Collectables Emporium, one of the two shops on the ground floor of Phyllis's apartment block.

From somewhere in the back of the long, narrow premises Mrs Lowerblast's voice shot back, 'Ah! *Guten tag*, Phyllis.'

Daisy, down by Phyllis's ankles, gave a short, sharp bark.

'And you too, Daisy, dear,' called Mrs Lowerblast.

A little noise came from the back of Daisy's throat (it sounded like she was quietly gargling with marbles in her mouth), and she trotted off to a patch of multi-coloured sunlight that was shining onto the floor through the stained-glass windows at the front of the shop. Here she lay down on her stomach and proceeded to lick her brown and white paws earnestly.

'Are you busy?' called Phyllis.

'Never too busy for you, my dear, never for you. Just give me two seconds, *ja*?'

'Okay.'

Phyllis peered around the dimly lit shop. It was crammed full of everything, its cedar display cabinets and shelves filled with porcelain figurines and silver jewellery and tea services; exquisite Fabergé eggs; vintage clockwork toys; strange pots and vases upon which lizards, birds and small, strange, unrecognisable creatures had been sculpted; rare coins; fancy bird cages hanging from the ceiling; boxes of used postcards that had been sent all around the world in the days when writing to someone was not an instantaneous process; hats and handbags from the 1920s; walking sticks with gold and silver handles, sometimes in the shape of dogs' or ducks' heads; brass telescopes of many different sizes; glaring tribal masks from islands that Phyllis had never heard of; boxes of unusual, long out-of-print magazines with titles like *A World of Ocelots* and *Better Yurts and Gardens* and *Don't Go There* and *Bagpipes for Beginners* and *Kenneth!*; and items of Victorian lace—shawls, handkerchiefs, tablecloths and what Mrs Lowerblast referred to as 'unmentionables'.

Phyllis always liked coming in here. She felt a sense of belonging amongst all the seemingly almost forgotten objects.

She ran her long fingers up and down the wooden edge of the counter. The smell of linseed oil, mingled with the slightly sweet fragrance of old things and the whiff of cobwebs (*do cobwebs have a smell?* wondered Phyllis), wafted up to her nostrils.

From far back in the shop, behind the dark purple curtain that separated the private area from the public, there came a few *mmm*s, and some low grunts and the sound of boxes being moved. Then the curtain was flung aside, and Mrs Lowerblast appeared, smiling at her young friend.

Phyllis smiled back and watched Mrs Hildegard Lowerblast come to the counter. She was an elderly woman, large in proportion and gentle in manner, who always wore her lustrous hair tied back in a neat, stylish ponytail.

Mrs Lowerblast had a great passion for objects from the past. Over the years she had taught Phyllis how old things—things that many people discarded or destroyed without thinking—more often than not told a story. And, according to Mrs Lowerblast, those stories, no matter how small they might be, were the threads that held together the blanket of history.

Phyllis had always liked that idea, and she had learnt much from her gently spoken friend.

But this afternoon Phyllis detected a cloud of concern that seemed to shadow Mrs Lowerblast's face, despite her smile.

'What's wrong?' Phyllis asked, always one to get to the point.

'Oh, my dear girl,' said Mrs Lowerblast, taking out a lilacious-coloured handkerchief from the bosom of her deep mauve dress (Mrs Lowerblast had a thing for the purple hues) and dabbing it across her forehead. 'You can read me like a book, you can.'

'Something's bothering you,' Phyllis said. 'What's happened?'

With a small grunt, Mrs Lowerblast hoisted herself onto the tall swivelling chair which was always behind the counter, perfectly positioned so that she could see every inch of the shop around her. 'Oh, Phyllis, my dear. I have been robbed!'

'No!'

Daisy stopped licking her paws and looked up, her ear (the one that was not permanently folded over) turning in the direction of Phyllis's voice.

'*Ja*.' Mrs Lowerblast nodded.

'Robbed?' repeated Phyllis.

Mrs Lowerblast gave a big, heaving sigh. 'In all the years I've had my business here in your building, I have never once been burglarised or even shoplifted. No *theftacious* activity has ever crossed my threshold! But now—' She dabbed at her neck with the handkerchief and frowned. 'Now my record, it is broken . . . shatterised, *kaput*!'

'Have you called the police?'

'*Nein*, my dear. It is not so straightforward.'

Now it was Phyllis's turn to frown. 'What do you mean?'

Mrs Lowerblast sighed again. 'I'll show you.' She swivelled her chair around and reached over to the far end of the counter, where she had a small mahogany and glass display cabinet on the counter-top. Phyllis knew Mrs Lowerblast kept some of her most valuable pieces in the cabinet.

She watched as the elderly woman opened the

back of the cabinet. From inside it she withdrew an object: a bookend, which she placed on the counter in front of Phyllis. Then she took out another one, a matching piece to the first, and put it side-by-side with its twin.

For some reason, Phyllis had never seen the bookends before. 'Wow,' she whispered, pushing her long, dark hair back behind her ears. 'They're beautiful!'

'Ah, you have always appreciated things of quality,' said Mrs Lowerblast. 'You have a fine eye, *ja*.'

Daisy sprang to her paws and trotted over to the counter. She was the sort of dog who always liked to know what was going on. She stood on her rear legs and tapped a front paw on Phyllis's knee. Phyllis bent down to pick her up, and together they looked at the bookends.

They were indeed beautiful. Phyllis's eyes widened as she took in every detail of them. They were L-shaped and were made of earthenware that had been fired in a kiln and glossily glazed. The colours were vibrant: against a dark brown background there were splashes of burnt orange, apple green, soft butter yellow, ochre and some streaks of deep blue. The bookends had been made to resemble the trunks of old, gnarled trees with knot-holes and ridges running down them.

On the front of each of the bookends, so lifelike that they seemed as if they were about to turn their heads, perched two small blue wrens. Their tails were raised against the bookends' uprights, and their spindly little legs were splayed out so that they were able to stand on the bases of the bookends. The expression on each bird's face was one of alertness, as though it had just heard a sound—a twig breaking, Phyllis was imagining—and was considering whether it should take flight, or remain where it was, suspended in time.

Daisy pushed her snout forward, had a sniff of the ceramic birds and then, deciding that they weren't food, she lost interest. Phyllis put her down on the floor and the small dog went and curled up in the kaleidoscopic sunlight again.

Phyllis kept staring at the bookends, taking in every colour and detail. For a few silent-as-an-empty-cathedral moments she felt that she was the same size as the wrens, on the tree trunk with them, in their world, hearing their sounds and smelling the forest around them.

'They are *extremely* valuable,' said Mrs Lowerblast, breaking the spell. 'Made by an Australian potter, about . . . oooooh . . . eighty years ago. We in the trade believe that there are only three sets of them left anywhere in the world.

The rare blue wren bookends made by the reclusive Gladys Reyscombe.'

Phyllis blinked. She was a little startled to find that her palms had left perspiration marks on the glass countertop. 'What do they have to do with you being robbed?' she asked.

Mrs Lowerblast shook her head slowly. 'It's all so strange, my dear. All so . . . *weird*. So peculiar-acious. Someone—lord knows *who*, and lord knows *how*—took one of these!'

Phyllis raised her eyebrows. 'You mean, you had three of them?'

'*Nein*. Just the two.'

'Huh?' Phyllis looked at Mrs Lowerblast, then at the two bookends, then back to Mrs Lowerblast. She knew her friend often got through her days in the shop with the help of rich fruit cake and the occasional glass of good sherry, and Phyllis wondered whether the fruit cake had perhaps run out and whether Mrs Lowerblast had only had her other favourite on hand lately . . .

'Let me get this straight,' said Phyllis (using one of her favourite phrases from an old film in which her great-grandfather had appeared many years ago). 'Somebody stole one of these blue wren bookends from you. You had two, and somebody stole *one*. And now you only have . . . *two*!

Mrs L., Maths may not be my best subject, but even *I* don't see how this adds up! Two minus one is one, unless they've changed the syllabus again . . .'

'I told you it was weird,' said Mrs Lowerblast. 'And now it gets weirder. You see, they *did* steal one of these, and they substituted it with a fake! I'm as certain of it as I am of my own elbows.' She pushed one of the blue wren bookends towards Phyllis. 'That, my dear, is not the work of the reclusive Gladys Reyscombe. That one is a modern-day knock-off! *Ja*!'

Phyllis scrutinised it carefully. 'But . . . it looks exactly the same as the other one. Are you sure?'

In answer, Mrs Lowerblast pointed her elbows at Phyllis and raised her eyebrows.

Phyllis reached for the bookends. 'May I?'

'Be my guest. Oh, this is a terrible business, Phyllis. Most horridacious. I bought the pair about three years ago . . . found them in a small market when I was travelling through the south of France. Snapped them up for a song—the sellers didn't know what they had! Do you know what they're valued at? What I can get for them? I'll tell you: at least forty thousand dollars!'

Phyllis looked up, her mouth open.

'*Ja*, an astonishing price. Anything made by Gladys Reyscombe always fetches top money, on account of the lovely work she did and the scarcity of it. And, according to many in the trade, the blue wren bookends were the final pieces she ever sculpted.

'But now, because I've only got *one* of the pieces, why, I'd guess it wouldn't be worth a quarter of that. Not that a quarter of forty thousand dollars is a sum to blow one's nose at, of course. But . . . oh, dear me . . .'

Phyllis had picked up the supposed fake bookend while Mrs Lowerblast had been speaking, and she had been running her fingers across all the ridges and surfaces, gently tracing the little bird's shape and tail. Now she put the bookend down and picked up the other one.

After a few moments she said, 'I can't feel any difference, Mrs L. They feel like the same weight, and their proportions are almost identical. Not exact, but close.'

'Mmmm. The originals weren't carbon copies of each other, of course, on account of them being hand-sculpted. Gladys Reyscombe never worked from moulds.'

Phyllis put the bookend down. 'Are you sure that when you bought them in the south of France, you didn't actually buy a genuine one and a fake one?' she asked respectfully.

'Positive, my dear. But that's why I haven't gone to the police. They'd ask me the same thing, just like that. They'd probably think, "Oh, she's just a funny old bat and she's starting to imagine things that didn't happen." Well, I may be getting on, *ja*, but all the marbles are still rolling around up here.' She tapped her forehead and sighed again. 'I know what I bought. I've been in this business long enough to smell a fake a mile off. I can easily detect the whiffaciousness of a forgery!'

'I'm sorry, I didn't mean to—'

Mrs Lowerblast gave a sad smile and patted Phyllis's hand. '*Nein*, *nein*. No offence taken, Phyllis. Of course you didn't. You know me. The police don't.'

'But how could this have happened?' asked Phyllis.

'Now this is the truly bizarre bit, my dear. My shop was never broken into. That cabinet—' she pointed to the small display case on the end of the counter—'is always locked, and the lock has never been tampered with. And I keep all the keys to all the locks on all the display cabinets in the safe out the back. The safe which, likewise, has never been broken into. On top of that, I've got the whole place alarmed. And no alarms have gone off that I know of in the last fifteen years.'

Mrs Lowerblast leant across the countertop. She looked all around, and then she gazed steadily at her young friend. '*Nein*, Phyllis, my dear,' she said in a hushed tone, 'I believe something very strange happened. I believe that it was done *right before my very eyes, and I had no idea what was being perpetrated!*'

Phyllis's spine tingled at this astonishing anouncement, sending a shudder throughout her entire being.

The substitution

'Before I tell you any more,' Mrs Lowerblast said, 'let me show you something.' She climbed down from the swivel chair. 'Excuse me a moment. I need some hot water to demonstrate this.'

She made her way to the back of the shop, stopping before she came to the dark purple curtain. With a small flourish she took out a gold pocket-watch from her breast pocket. 'Ah, will you look at the ticker? Time to close for the day. Phyllis, would you mind doing the honours? You know the drill, *ja*?'

'Right away, Mrs L.'

Mrs Lowerblast disappeared behind the curtain while Phyllis closed the front door, clicked the three locks over and turned the OPEN sign around so that it read CLOSED to all the world outside—the bustling swarm of people hurrying to the subways and bus stops and carparks, leaving the bright lights of the city to return to their homes.

'Look at them, Daisy,' said Phyllis, watching through the stained-glass panels in the old door. 'All of them crowding and rushing. I'm glad we don't have far to travel home every day.'

Daisy looked up, her dark eyes glowing like shiny brown marbles.

Phyllis kept watching the throngs outside. She enjoyed observing people going about their lives. Sometimes she'd hang out with her friend Clement in City Park and, while he was always mucking about with his latest webPad or newest cell phone or whatever just-released piece of electronic gadgetry his parents had given him (they owned one of the biggest electronics stores in the city), Phyllis would just sit there, or lie on her stomach on the grass, watching everything around her.

She always found a special sort of happy calmness when she did this. Almost as happy as when she was performing a magic trick for her friends.

'*Danke*, my dear.'

Phyllis jumped—she'd been so engrossed in her scrutinising, she hadn't realised that Mrs Lowerblast was back at the counter. Mrs Lowerblast put a big mug of boiling water onto the countertop and sat heavily in the chair. She opened a drawer by her knees and took out a long silver darning needle.

'I just want to show you this now, Phyllis, so that you're convinced. This is how I found out the bookend was a fake.' She dipped the needle into the mug of boiling water and held it there for a few seconds. 'If you don't mind,' she said, 'would you upturn that one—' she indicated the bookend closest to Phyllis, the one she believed was the fake—'so that the underside of the base is showing?'

Carefully, Phyllis did as she was asked, trying not to damage the delicate wings, legs and beak of the sculpted blue wren.

'Now,' Mrs Lowerblast said, 'watch this.'

She took the needle out of the boiling water and placed one hand around the base of the bookend. Then, quickly and smoothly, she put the tip of the needle to the underside of the base and pushed it.

The needle slid cleanly in, all the way to Mrs Lowerblast's fingertips.

Phyllis frowned and looked at her friend. 'That shouldn't happen, should it?' she asked. 'I mean, these are heavy and they're made of clay that's been heated and fired, so it should be rock hard . . . we did pottery in Art at school last year . . .'

Mrs Lowerblast withdrew the needle. '*Ja*, that's right. But this one isn't clay. This one's *plaster*. Whereas the *other* one . . .' She dipped the needle back into the boiling water, held it there for a few moments and said, 'Do the honours again, would you?'

Phyllis took the other bookend and gently turned it over so that the underside was displayed.

Mrs Lowerblast passed the needle to Phyllis. 'Your turn. Careful, dear, it's hot. Now, see if you can stick it into that one . . .'

Phyllis held the needle, tentatively pressed the tip against the bookend, and pushed.

Nothing. The needle would not penetrate.

'And *that*,' declared Mrs Lowerblast, 'is a genuine blue wren bookend by Gladys Reyscombe.'

'Well, there's no doubt about it,' said Phyllis. 'That other one's a pretender, all right.'

Mrs Lowerblast smiled sadly. 'I have been hoodwinkled! Right before my very eyeballs . . .'

Phyllis shuddered again. 'How do you mean?'

'He did it when he was here. It *must* have been him. Standing right there in front of me. But how he did it, well, for the dear life of me, I cannot figure it out at all.'

Phyllis's eyes narrowed. 'He? Who? Who's he? You must tell me!'

Mrs Lowerblast took out her lilacious handkerchief and touched it to the corners of her lavender-lipsticked mouth. 'Oh, Phyllis, I've gone over it a hundred times in my head, maybe two hundred times. I've tried to remember every single thing that happened when he visited and looked at the bookends, every little detail. But I still can't work out how he substituted this for the genuine article!'

'Mrs L.! Who is this *he*?'

Mrs Lowerblast leant closer and spoke in a low tone across the blue wren bookends. 'The man in the frock coat!'

'Frock coat?'

'*Ja*. A dark blue frock coat with a velvet collar. The sort of thing they used to wear at the beginning of last century and the end of the century before that. You don't see them worn much nowadays. But nothing surprises me, Phyllis . . . I get all types of people in here, wearing all sorts of clothes . . .'

'Do you know his name?'

'*Nein*. *Nein*, I never thought to ask. I usually only find out a customer's name when they make a purchase and I write out a receipt for them. And this man certainly didn't *purchase* from me!'

Phyllis put her elbows on the counter and cupped her chin in her hands. 'When did he come in?'

'Oh, it wasn't just the once. He came in four times. About three months ago. But it was only yesterday when I was dusting the bookends that I smelled a rat.'

'Four times? So you got a good look at him, then?'

'Mmmm.' Mrs Lowerblast pulled a face, as though she had just sat in jelly or something squirm-making. 'Funny-looking man. Tall, thin, not that old, with pinched features. And dark hair, lots of it, combed back off his forehead, long at the back, falling on his shoulders. He had full lips, almost *pouty* lips—I remember thinking they wouldn't look out of place on a supermodel. And he had this scar—' she ran her finger from the inside corner of her eye in a diagonal line to halfway down her cheek—'just like that. Sort of pale reddish-brown, it was.'

Phyllis listened intently, storing the details away in her mind.

'And he wore a monocle. A *monocle*, Phyllis! No one wears a monocle these days. But I must admit, it didn't surprise me. Some of my customers are very wealthy and . . . well, I guess, *eccentric*. He just seemed like that sort of customer.'

'What did he do when he came in?'

'Ah, like I said, I remember every detail. He'd approach the counter and bid me a good afternoon—he always came late in the day, never in the mornings or early afternoons. He had a crisp tone to his voice, which was deep but not unpleasant.

He'd stand there, right where you are now, and ask to see the Reyscombe blue wren bookends.

'Well, the first time I showed them to him he just looked for what seemed like minutes. Never uttered a word. He didn't even touch them. Then, finally, he looked up at me and gave a curt nod. Just one. He picked up his bag and said he'd have a think about them. Then he left.'

'He had a bag?' Phyllis took her elbows off the counter and straightened.

'*Ja*. Always came with it. A tallish sort of . . . oblong-shaped leather bag with a handle at the top. Black leather. Sort of like a briefcase, but taller and not as wide. He always put it on the counter to the left of him.'

Phyllis bit her bottom lip. 'Did he ever open it in front of you?'

'Never.' Mrs Lowerblast folded her arms across her bosoms. 'It always remained closed.'

Daisy had fallen asleep in the steadily fading patch of sunlight that was now shining feebly through the stained-glass windows. Her tiny snores wafted around the place like wispy, feathery gruntings.

'What about the next time he came in?' asked Phyllis. 'What happened then?'

'Same thing to start. In he comes, "Good

afternoon," he says, putting his bag down there, and he asks to see the bookends again. Ever so politely, even if he was a bit abrupt. So I got them out and placed them on the display mat there in front of him. This time he asked if he could hold them. Well, I let him—his hands were fine, such long, delicate fingers, like a pianist's. I just assumed he'd treat them delicately, which he did. He picked up one, then the other.

'And he did something with his hand, Phyllis. He extended his middle finger and stretched it away from his thumb as far as it would go. Then he held his splayed hand along the length of the base, almost as if he were measuring it . . .'

'What did he do next?'

'Well, he said to me that he still wasn't sure. He said he could certainly afford the forty-thousand-dollar price tag, but he needed to think about whether they would *fit into his collection.* I understood what he was saying; sometimes people buy pieces from me and then they get them home and the pieces are totally out of place with everything else they have at home. Their fine arts collection suddenly looks like a fine dog's breakfast. So they return the pieces and I give them a store credit. Well anyway, he bade me farewell, picked up his bag and off he went.'

'Okay. Anything different happen on the third visit?'

'That time he asked if he could *photograph* the bookends. He said he wanted to print out the photo and put it amongst his other pieces of rare pottery in his home, just to see if everything would go together. Well, because he'd been back three times by this stage I thought he was genuine in his interest and getting closer to buying them, so I agreed. I got the bookends out, put them on the counter, and he repositioned them, first that one, then the other. He took his camera out of his bag and moved the bag off the counter, to give him more room for the photo. And—snap! Off went the flash and he smiled with those pouty lips, and thanked me very much and said he'd be back within a day or two to let me know whether he'd buy or not.'

'And then he left?'

'That he did, Phyllis.'

'And the bookends were exactly where he'd put them?'

'*Ja*. That was the last time he handled them. I put them away again after he'd gone, just like normal. And then, true to his word, two days later, just before I was about to close for the day, in he comes. He tells me that he's considered it all carefully, but he's decided not to go ahead with the purchase. Well, I thank him and then he starts to leave. But before he goes, Phyllis, he stops, only for a moment, and he stares at the blue wren bookends in the display case there. And I'll never to my dying day forget the look on his face: the corners of his pouty lips curled up, and his eyes seemed to *glow bright green*! Not the irises or the pupils, but the white bits.'

Phyllis's stomach did a flip-flop.

'Ooooh, it gave me the heebie-jeebies, I can tell you.'

'Hmm.' Phyllis ran her thumb across her lower lip. 'Mrs L., has anyone else looked at the bookends during the last few months?'

'Ah, no, my dear. He was the only one showing any interest. I think the price I am asking put others off . . .'

Phyllis frowned. *This is whacky*, she thought. *Why would he just steal one? Why not both? And why, if he* had *somehow substituted the fake on one of his visits, didn't he substitute* both *of them? But how did he pull it off? She was watching him the whole time . . .*

Mrs Lowerblast inspected her gold pocket-watch. 'Oh, my giddilacious aunty! Look at the time. You'd best be hurrying upstairs before your father gets home.'

At the sound of the word 'upstairs', Daisy woke from her half-slumber. She stood, yawned and padded across to Phyllis's ankles.

'Oh, Phyllis,' said Mrs Lowerblast, 'before you go, how about a little prestidigitation?'

Phyllis blinked. 'What? Oh, sure.' She smiled and fished a copper coin out of her jeans pocket. 'Watch carefully, my good Mrs Lowerblast.'

She held the coin between her index finger and thumb, and displayed the empty palm of her other hand. Then she slowly placed the coin into her palm and wrapped the fingers of that hand around it.

'Gold or silver, Mrs L.? What do you like best?'

'Ooooh, silver!'

Phyllis blew into her hand and then slowly opened her fingers. There, instead of the copper coin, was a gleaming silver half-dollar.

Phyllis handed the coin to her friend. 'For you,' she said to the smiling woman. She scooped up Daisy and unlocked the front door. 'See you soon, Mrs L. And don't worry—I'm going to look into the mystery of the fake bookend!'

Croissants and Clement

The next morning Phyllis texted her friend Clement and asked him to meet her by their statue in City Park at 10:30.

(Well, it wasn't technically *their* statue . . . they hadn't paid for it or anything, or arranged to have it placed there. It was just one of their usual meeting points. With both Phyllis and Clement being city dwellers, they had a number of regular places around town where they met up. The statue itself was of some long-forgotten politician with a big bronze beard and a portly stomach, who was carrying what appeared to be a weasel under one of his arms. Why he was carrying a weasel, nobody knew any more.)

Clement texted back almost straightaway to say yes, he'd be there. Anything to get out of xylophone practice.

On the way Phyllis and Daisy called in to have a quick bite to eat at The Délicieux Café. The small café was one of Phyllis's favourite places for three reasons:

1. It served the BEST cakes and croissants of all the cafés in the city.
2. The owners, Pascaline and Pierre Ravissant, always made Phyllis and Daisy welcome, and were always eager to see Phyllis's latest feat of legerdemain.
3. It was on the ground floor of Phyllis's apartment block, separated from Lowerblast's Antiques & Collectables Emporium by the entrance to the lobby.

This morning when Phyllis and Daisy entered The Délicieux Café Pascaline called out from the coffee machine, 'Ah! *Bonjour*, Phyllees. Your usual table awaits you!'

'Morning, Pascaline.' Phyllis and Daisy went to one of the two tables that were nestled in the small bay windows at the front of the café. This was one of Phyllis's best places to watch passers-by.

'Pierre!' called Pascaline. 'Your favourite girl apart from me is 'ere.'

'Ah-ha! Ze conjuror 'as returned!' From out of the kitchen came Pierre, wiping his hands on a white teatowel that hung from his long white apron.

'Hello,' Phyllis greeted him and sat at the table. Daisy gave a small, high-pitched yap before settling herself at Phyllis's feet.

'*Bonjour*, Phyllees, 'allo, leetle derg.' Pierre stood to the side of the table and addressed Phyllis over his right shoulder. 'So . . . ze usual for you, mademoiselle?' (He had an unusual way of talking to people over his right shoulder, which came in handy when he was waiting on tables—it gave him a commanding, more dignified presence, he thought. This was a good thing for a man in his profession.)

'Yes please,' said Phyllis.

'Wern chocolate croissant and 'ot chocolate will ernly be a bertterfly's breath away,' said Pierre.

Phyllis giggled and off he went.

The only other customer in the café was a man sitting at one of the tables against the wall, reading the entertainment section of the almost-as-thick-as-a-brick Saturday newspaper.

'So,' Pascaline called to Phyllis, 'what's on for today?'

'Just hanging out,' Phyllis replied. 'Meeting Clement in about half an hour in the park.'

'Ah. 'Ow is Clem? We have nert seen 'im for a while.'

'Oh, you know. He's just Clement. He's got a new phone, so you can barely get a sensible word out of him at the moment.'

Pascaline smiled as she busied herself at the coffee machine.

'And tonight,' Phyllis said, 'Dad and I are going to watch one of Great-grandfather's movies. It's the anniversary of his . . . *disappearance* today.'

'Ah,' said Pierre over his shoulder as he set down the chocolate croissant and hot chocolate on Phyllis's table. 'Ze great Wallace Wong, Conjuror erf Wonder, eh?'

'The one and only.' Phyllis smiled. 'Thank you, Pierre.'

'Zink nerthing erf eet. I dern't.' With that he winked, twitched his neat, thin moustache and hurried back to the kitchen.

Pascaline delivered a coffee to the man reading the newspaper and then came over to Phyllis. 'He merst 'ave been incredible, merstn't he, your great-grandfather? To zink, he made zo merch money zat 'e was able to build zis very building. Right een ze centre erf ze city 'ere!'

Phyllis took a sip of her hot chocolate. 'Mmm. It couldn't happen today. Way back then magicians were as famous as the biggest rock stars are now. They were huge. But then the movies got more popular and things changed. People started going to the pictures, not the live shows so much. But Great-grandfather was smart, all right. He went over to Hollywood and started getting into the movies. I'm glad he did, because if he hadn't, I wouldn't be able to see him performing his magic today.'

'Preserved fer posterity,' said Pascaline.

'Yep,' said Phyllis. 'Preserved for posterity.' She looked out through the side of the bay window at Mrs Lowerblast's closed shop (she never opened on the weekends). Then she asked Pascaline, 'Have you spoken to Mrs L. lately?'

'Oh, *oui*, I was chatting wiz 'er yesterday morning. Serch an 'orrible business wiz zerm berkends, she told me abert. Do you know erf zis?'

'Yes,' Phyllis said between mouthfuls of her croissant. 'I saw her yesterday afternoon.'

Pascaline dusted the back of the empty chair opposite Phyllis. 'You dern't zink she 'as made a leetle . . . *mistake*? Zat per'aps she was *nert* robbed, bert 'ad zese two pieces all alerng? You dern't zink zat, maybe, she ees a beet *merddled*?'

Phyllis frowned. She felt protective of Mrs Lowerblast. Phyllis knew that Mrs L. had not got muddled about the bookends. In Phyllis's opinion a serious crime had been committed.

'No, Pascaline. Mrs L. was definitely robbed.'

Pascaline shook her head. 'Eet ees nert good, Phyllis. Nert good at erll . . .'

Just then a couple came into the café. Pascaline smiled at Phyllis, excused herself and went to show the new customers to a table.

You're telling me, thought Phyllis as she finished up her delicious pastry.

'Never heard of her,' said Clement, pushing his glasses back up the bridge of his nose as the fingers on his other hand darted across the screen of his new phone like a startled octopus's tentacles across the ocean floor.

'Mrs L. said she was a recluse,' said Phyllis. 'That's partly why her ceramics are so valuable. She didn't make all that much, and the bookends are supposed to be the last things she did.'

Daisy was off-leash, sniffing around at the big stone base of the politician with the weasel. Phyllis, lying on her stomach on the warm grass, was keeping a close eye on her.

'How do you spell it?' Clement asked.

Phyllis thought. 'Try R-E-Y-S-C-O-M-B-E. I've never seen it written down.'

'Let's Google her.' Clement entered the letters and waited a few seconds. 'Yep, that's right. She's here. Gladys Reyscombe. Died in 1956.'

'And . . . ?'

'Just going to her entry. Ha. Not much there.'

'What does it say?'

Clement's glasses had slid down his nose again, so he pushed them back up (he'd only just got them—his last pair had broken the week before when he had walked into a lamppost while reading something on his webPad). '"Australian potter",' he read aloud. '"Active 1925–1956. Remembered chiefly for her realistic depictions of Australian birds and marsupials." And that's it.'

'Nothing else?'

'Nup.'

'Try searching blue wren bookends.'

Clement looked at her, then typed in the words. 'Let's do an image search,' he said. After a few seconds he pulled his head back. 'Oo-er!' he gasped, his cheeks turning red.

'What?'

His eyes went big and he started to giggle.

'Let's see!' Phyllis reached over and grabbed the phone from him. She looked at the image being displayed of two identical women, standing back-to-back, wearing big blue feathers and not much else. '"Latrice and Lavinia, twins of the tightrope!",' she read. '"Available for corporate events and functions. If you want your business looking up, look us up first!"'

Clement smirked.

Phyllis switched off the phone abruptly. 'That's not the sort of blue wren bookends we want,' she said.

'We?'

She rolled over onto her back and watched the faint wispy clouds floating by. 'This is a mystery, Clem. Somehow a man stole something from right in front of Mrs L. and swapped it with something else, and she never saw a thing. I'm going to try and work it out. And you're going to help me.'

'Me? Hey! When did you ask if I *wanted* to help you? What if I have other things to do?'

She smiled. 'You always have other things to do. But you still always manage to help me, don't you? Hey, it'll be more fun than xylophone practice, won't it?' She looked at him and winked.

Clement blushed and pushed up his glasses. (Whether he liked to admit it or not, he did like spending time with Phyllis Wong, even if she was a girl and even if she was a year and ten days older than him.) 'Yeah . . . well . . . I guess I'll help,' he stammered.

'Good.' Phyllis rolled back onto her stomach and propped her chin in her hands.

'Where are you going to start?' Clement asked.

‘I mean, *we*.’ He sighed. ‘Where are *we* going to start?’

Daisy came bouncing across the grass. Her little tail wagged happily as she bounced up and down on Phyllis’s back. ‘Now *that*,’ Phyllis said, ‘is a very good question . . .’

An appointment with the floorboards

The Wallace Wong Building, as it is known today, was built in 1932 and is a beautiful example of Art Deco architecture. So beautiful, in fact, that at various times throughout the year, tour groups of Art Deco architecture fans visit the building to photograph it and gaze in admiration at its clean lines and curved glass windows.

It is not a large building; it is only three storeys tall from the street, with an underground basement which makes it four storeys, and it is not very wide. The street level has Mrs Lowerblast's emporium and the Ravissants' café, which are positioned on either side of the impressive glass-and-chromium doors which lead into the small but opulent lobby.

In the lobby is an elevator with wooden doors decorated with inlaid stars and comets and a few of the more picturesque planets from various galaxies. A narrow staircase with a detailed, scrolled chrome balustrade (featuring birds and giraffes and Art

Deco–style women with flowing, crimped hair) rises up from the sumptuously tiled lobby floor to the apartments above.

There are five apartments in the Wallace Wong Building: four on the first floor and a very spacious apartment which covers the entire top level. This is where Phyllis and Daisy live with Phyllis's father. Above that is a small rooftop terrace where Mr Wong has a glasshouse, in which he tries to grow rare orchids and insect-eating plants of some exoticism. Unfortunately, Mr Wong is often away on business, so the plants do not have a great rate of survival.

When Wallace Wong had the building erected it was surrounded by apartment blocks of similar height and proportion. But over the years all of the original neighbouring structures have gone; torn down to make way for skyscrapers that thrust upwards with cold disregard for the sort of elegance that Wallace Wong put into the design of his building.

Phyllis's father inherited the property from his father, who had inherited it from the Conjuror of Wonder after his disappearance. Phyllis's father has turned down many offers to buy the Wallace Wong Building, and it now remains, hemmed in and surrounded by these skyscrapers of glass and steel and cold reflections, a small reminder of a time when the world welcomed a different sort of style.

Phyllis and her father had just cooked a delicious dinner of ocean salmon in a light lemon sauce, with steamed potatoes and asparagus. This was followed by a white peach soufflé, which they had ordered up from The Délicieux Café. Phyllis and her dad usually took turns cooking the evening meal—both of them enjoyed doing it, and their kitchen was well-equipped, so there were seldom any dramas about it—but on Saturday nights they shared the job.

This was one of Phyllis's favourite times of the week. She liked working alongside her dad, chopping and dicing, sautéing and steaming. Mr Wong never talked about business on Saturday nights, and they always shared the cleaning up afterwards.

On some Saturday nights (like tonight), they would open up the small cinema, still in its original plush condition at the end of the hallway at the back of their apartment, and screen one of the movies that Wallace Wong had appeared in.

The cinema was like a glorious hidden cave in the apartment. There was a soundproof projection room at the rear and a high, domed ceiling in which hundreds of tiny electric globes sparkled against the dark, almost midnight-blue of the dome. To sit in there was like sitting in the open air, underneath the most dazzling, star-studded sky.

The walls were as they had been painted in 1932: realistic scenes of rolling hills and ancient, crumbling temples that stretched far away into the distance. These could be glimpsed between the wooden, inlaid columns that were spaced along the walls.

At the far end of the auditorium a heavy burgundy velvet curtain trimmed with crimson edging and golden tassels concealed the movie screen. The velvet curtain was motorised to open at exactly the right time during screenings. Mr Wong controlled such procedures from the projection room at the rear.

To the right of the curtain was a bronze-framed display case mounted on the wall. Inside this were various bold posters featuring *Wallace Wong—Conjuror of Wonder!* In the posters he was busy performing such illusions as levitating an enormous Egyptian sphinx, sawing not one but *two* women in half at the same time, producing dozens of alarm clocks from a small silk purse on a long handle, and even bringing forth a Bengal tiger from a floating sphere. A few posters for some of Wallace

Wong's movies were also on display with the magic posters.

Tonight Phyllis sat with Daisy on her lap in one of the sumptuous armchairs in the auditorium, waiting while her father prepared the film for the projector in the projection room. The plump armchairs in the cinema were so soft and enveloping that Phyllis often felt like she was a silkworm in a cosy (but slightly dusty) cocoon when she sank into one.

Phyllis's dad peeked out through the window in the projection room's wall. 'How about *An Appointment With The Floorboards** tonight?' he asked.

'Sounds good,' Phyllis said. 'We haven't seen that for a while.'

'Okeydokey,' said her father.

'Have we, Daisy?' Phyllis stroked Daisy's ears—one up, one permanently folded—as the little terrier delicately licked her paws. Every now and then she would raise a freshly-licked paw and

---

* *An Appointment With The Floorboards* (Supreme Pictures, 1930). This detective thriller marked Wallace Wong's (Conjuror of Wonder!) first known Hollywood film appearance. He appears in a nightclub scene as an illusionist, and was cast because of his expertise in sawing people asunder and putting them back together again. His small performance led to bigger roles, eventually culminating in the lead role in *No Time For Neddy* (1936). *(Information supplied by P.B. Botter, film historian.)*

use it to wash her snout, first one side and then the other.

Through the projection room window Mr Wong could hear the little squealy noises Daisy made whenever she was thus engaged. 'I swear that dog was brought up by a cat, Phyll,' he said, laughing.

'I wonder,' Phyllis said. Her father usually made that observation about once a month, and Phyllis nearly always said 'I wonder' when he did. The truth of the matter was that neither of them knew much about Daisy's background. She was a rescue dog, obtained from the pound by Mr Wong and given to Phyllis as a present for her tenth birthday. Phyllis and her dad spoiled her to bits, but Daisy didn't act like a spoiled dog. She was always loving and trusting and would bark protectively if she sensed—rightly or wrongly—that Phyllis was in some sort of bother.

'Dad?'

'Mm? What, love?'

'Have you spoken to Mrs Lowerblast lately?'

'No, Phyll. Not in weeks.' Mr Wong was not an in-your-face landlord, and he rarely saw Mrs Lowerblast or the Ravissants, except for a brief hello if he were passing by. 'How is she?' he asked, threading one end of a large reel of film into the old movie projector.

'Something strange has happened, Dad . . .'

He stopped threading the film and came out into the auditorium. 'Tell me,' he said, sitting in the armchair next to Phyllis and Daisy.

So Phyllis told him all about the mystery of the blue wren bookends.

Mr Wong listened carefully. Occasionally he would say something like, 'A frock coat? Goodness me . . .' or 'Always in the afternoons, eh?' or 'Almost identical . . . how extraordinary,' and he always said these things in a thoughtful tone. Never once did he ask Phyllis if she thought Mrs Lowerblast might have been mistaken about the whole incident.

When Phyllis had finished, her father said, 'Well, Phyll, that's one of the weirdest things I've heard.'

'It's screwy, all right.'

Her dad smiled. 'Just as your great-grandfather might've put it. Yes, it is.'

'What should I do? I want to help her, Dad, but where do I start?'

Her father smiled as an idea came to him. 'Why not talk to Chief Inspector Inglis?' he asked. 'It sounds like this might be right up his alley.'

Phyllis stroked the back of Daisy's head. 'Chief Inspector Inglis,' she repeated, her eyes narrowing.

‘He’s always got time for you, Phyll. And he’s off-duty tomorrow.’

‘Good idea, Dad. I’ll see if I can catch him.’

‘It can’t do any harm to talk to him about it all. And now,’ said her father, getting up and heading back towards the projection room, ‘let’s watch your great-grandfather saw that little showgirl in half, shall we?’

Inspector Inglis is informed

Chief Inspector Barry Inglis was a detective with the City Central branch of the metropolitan police force. He lived by himself in one of the apartments on the first floor of the Wallace Wong Building, and Phyllis had known him since she was about five years old.

Phyllis always remembered their first meeting with a mixture of giggle-making pleasure and a little bit of horror. She had been playing with a ball and jump rope by herself on the stairs leading up from the lobby. She had tied the rope across the chrome balustrades so that it cut across the stairs at about knee-height, and was trying to throw the ball down the stairs, making it bounce on only one step before going under the jump rope and hitting the wall at the bottom of the stairs, where they turned the corner. She had discovered that if she bounced the ball hard enough, it would fly all the way back to her at the top landing of the stairs, where she would catch it and repeat the game.

She had soon got the knack of it and was absorbed in the game, when, unbeknown to her, Inspector Barry Inglis (he was not a Chief Inspector then) came home with his arms full of grocery bags. He was carrying the big paper bags against his chest, and his field of vision was not as clear as a detective of his calibre would have liked. It had been raining and he was wet and drizzled, and his big paper bags were a bit soggy.

As he turned the corner of the stairwell and proceeded up the stairs, he had no idea that little Phyllis was busy with her game of dexterity and skill. Upwards he climbed, grunting a little (for, as well as some fresh fruit and vegetables, he had lots of tinned foods in the grocery bags, and they were growing heavier by the second). He was looking forward to dumping the whole lot in his apartment and settling himself in front of the TV for the afternoon to watch the baseball.

Ahead of him loomed the jump rope.

Ahead of him sat Phyllis, unaware of his approach and ready to bounce the ball.

So involved was Phyllis in her game that she didn't see Barry Inglis coming up the stairs. To be fair, the lighting in the stairwell was what one might call 'ambient'—it cast a muted glow upon the finely designed chromework of the balustrade and the marble steps, but it wasn't really bright enough to read by.

Grunting quietly, Inspector Inglis climbed higher.

Her tongue poking out the edge of her mouth as she concentrated hard, Phyllis held the ball above her head.

And let it fly!

It hit the step Phyllis was aiming for and bounced under the rope, then up, straight into the grocery bags in front of Inspector Inglis's face. There was a loud *SPLART* sound.

Barry Inglis gave a grunt of surprise and reeled, staggering backwards down a few steps, the top half of his grocery-bag laden body bending this way and that as he tried to regain his balance. He turned, swayed and then, almost miraculously, he found that he had not fallen, but was still upright. Shaken, but upright.

He turned around and peered over the top of his shopping bags. As far as he could see the stairway ahead was empty.

Muttering under his breath, Inspector Inglis continued up the stairs.

But he hadn't seen the jump rope.

With a mighty CRASH he went straight down, like a ton of bricks intermingled with tinned food and fresh fruit and vegetables. Then, face-down and amid the rolling tins, he slid swiftly on his stomach, backwards under the rope, down, down, down the stairs, slithering, *ooof*ing and groaning all the way, and making a grunting sound that if it were words would have said, 'Why me? Of all the cops in this town, why me?'

He hit the wall at the landing, rolled over and sat there, stunned.

He remained there with his back to the wall, listening to his tins clattering down the stairs below him. He picked a squashed tomato off his wet coat, throwing it onto the steps with a SPLAT! He ran a hand through his sandy-coloured hair and when he brought it away he found it was sticky with a few pulverised grapes.

With a groan he realised that he was sitting in a puddle of runny eggs and splintered eggshells.

Then he became aware of a small face at the top of the stairs. He looked up at it and, despite the indignity of his mishap, he couldn't feel any anger. That little face reminded him of a small rabbit, its wide eyes totally without mischief.

'Hello,' said the owner of the little face. 'My name is Phyllis Wong. What's your name?'

Barry Inglis pulled a spear of squished asparagus from out of his right ear. 'Inglis,' he said, squirming. 'But you can call me Inspector.'

*

Now Phyllis was sitting on the same step from which Barry Inglis had taken his tumble all those years ago. She planned to nab him when he left his apartment to go to his Sunday morning game of tennis.

At 10:25 precisely, Barry's door opened and out he came, dressed in his whites. He was aged somewhere in his thirties, no longer a very young man, but nor was he very old. His hair was still sandy, with the tiniest flecks of grey appearing around the temples, and he had the sort of vibrant blue eyes that would ensure he would always have a youthful zest to him.

Sometimes, when Phyllis caught sight of him passing by on the sidewalk, he reminded her of someone from the movies; not one of the stars, but the ones who were always playing the more interesting character roles.

'Morning, Chief Inspector Inglis!' With a flash of her hand, Phyllis spread a deck of cards face-up across the step above her. 'Bet I can read your mind!'

'Ah, Miss Wong.' Chief Inspector Inglis gave an almost half-smile (Phyllis had never seen him give a full, wide smile . . . she had a theory that he had been taught at Detective School that to smile in such a way was not considered the proper thing for someone who solved crimes for a living). 'Will it take long?' he asked, checking his watch.

'No,' Phyllis promised.

The Chief Inspector came and sat on the step above where Phyllis had spread the deck. He placed his tennis racquet next to him on the step.

'Now,' she said, 'I have the power, Chief Inspector, to see into the very depths of your mind . . . into the very heart of your soul . . .'

Inspector Barry Inglis squirmed, but only slightly.

'. . . and,' she continued, 'I shall use this ordinary deck of cards to prove it.' She held out her hand, palm down, and waved it across the cards. 'Notice, Chief Inspector, that all the cards are different.'

'That they are.'

'If you will be so kind as to select one card and one card only from the deck. Then take it out and show me what it is.'

Barry Inglis frowned. 'But how are you going to read my mind if you already know what the card is?'

'I have already detected which card you will choose.'

Barry frowned some more. Sometimes Phyllis's magic put him on edge. He preferred cold, hard facts; things that could be proven. Sometimes he found her magic a bit . . . *spooky*. Not that he'd ever admit that to anyone.

'One card only,' Phyllis said.

'Okay then.' He took a breath and withdrew a card from the left-hand side of the splayed deck. 'There. The nine of diamonds.'

'The nine of diamonds,' Phyllis repeated.

'Yes,' said Barry Inglis.

Phyllis smiled at him, and the Inspector squirmed a bit more.

'Now,' Phyllis said, 'please replace the card anywhere in the deck.'

Barry slid it back into the fanned deck.

'Watch.' She waved her hands across the cards, closing them into a neat stack which she placed on her palm.

She turned the deck over and spread it out again on the step, this time with the backs of the cards facing up. All of the backs were ordinary; all of them had the exact same design.

Except for one. On one card, there was some handwriting on the back.

'Will you take that card out and read what it says, please?' Phyllis asked.

Barry Inglis took out the card and read aloud the words written on it in Phyllis's handwriting: '"I *knew* you would choose the nine of diamonds. Phyllis Wong."'

He looked at her, his mouth open. 'But how in the name of—?'

'Turn it over,' said Phyllis.

Inspector Inglis turned over the card. It was the nine of diamonds.

Phyllis had the special glint in her eyes she always got when she had just created a moment of mystery.

'Well, I'll be apprehended,' said Barry Inglis. 'You get more amazing every single time, you do.' He went to hand the card back to her.

'No, that's yours.' Phyllis scooped up the deck and put it in her pocket.

'Thanks.' The Chief Inspector picked up his tennis racquet and stood. 'I never fail to be astounded by you, Miss Wong. There's always something new. And there's the wonder of the thing. Thank you for that.' He popped the nine of diamonds into his pocket.

'My pleasure,' said Phyllis, standing up. 'May I walk with you for a bit?'

'I would be very glad if you did,' said Chief Inspector Inglis.

'I want to talk to you about something.'

'Oh, yes?' The Chief Inspector took big strides across the lobby and reached the doors before Phyllis. He held one of them open for her and she went out into the bright, warm sunshine. Barry followed and together they started walking towards the City Tennis Centre, which was a few blocks north of the Wallace Wong Building.

'It's about Mrs Lowerblast. She was robbed.'

Inspector Inglis's pace slowed, but only briefly. 'Did she tell you that?' he asked.

'Mm-hm. On Friday when I called in after school. She said it happened some time about three months ago.'

'Did she report it?'

'No. She only just realised this week.'

'But she still didn't report it?'

'No. She feels funny about it all.'

They arrived at the intersection at the corner of their block. Barry pushed the pedestrian button and they waited. 'What was taken?' he asked.

The lights changed and Phyllis filled him in on all that Mrs Lowerblast had told her as they crossed the street and headed towards the Tennis Centre.

After a few minutes Inspector Inglis stopped and looked at Phyllis. 'Right before her very eyes?' he said, repeating her words.

'That's what makes it so weird,' said Phyllis. 'She was there the whole time. She never left this guy alone in the shop, and she hasn't been broken into, and neither has the display cabinet where the bookends were kept.'

'Hmm,' Barry said. He started walking again.

'Can you talk to her, please?' Phyllis asked. 'Could you see her when she opens again to-morrow?'

The Chief Inspector's brow was furrowed. 'Yes, I guess I could. I could call in before I go to the station in the morning.'

'May I come too?'

He sighed. 'Well, I guess I can't stop you from being in Mrs Lowerblast's shop while I'm making my enquiries, can I?' he said. 'I'll be there about nine.'

'Peachy,' said Phyllis.

They had arrived at the Tennis Centre. 'And now,' Barry said, 'I thank you for your company and for this morning's entertainment. Good morning, Miss Wong.'

'See you, Inspector. Hope you win by a gazillion sets.'

'Thank you, Miss Wong. I fully intend to.'

Monday

'And you have no idea how this happened?' Chief Inspector Barry Inglis asked Mrs Lowerblast the next morning.

'No, she doesn't,' said Phyllis, standing at his elbow with Daisy by her ankles. 'Like she told you, he must have substituted it.'

'Miss Wong,' Barry said patiently, 'please allow Mrs Lowerblast to tell me.'

'Go on, Mrs L. Tell him.'

'*Ja*, Inspector Inglis. I have no idea. It is a total mystery to me.'

'And you never took your eyes off him?'

'Not for *ein* second. Even when I was getting the blue wrens out of the cabinet, he was within my area of glimpsing.'

Barry Inglis picked up the bookends which Mrs Lowerblast had got out to show him. He weighed them in both hands.

'Ah, please be careful with them. They are very valuable.'

'They sure are,' Phyllis piped up. 'A true pair's worth forty thousand dollars!'

'For the love of Mike,' the Inspector said. 'That's a lot of speeding fines, that is.'

'*Ja*, but now they are not worth anywhere near that,' said Mrs Lowerblast.

He put the bookends back onto the counter. He looked up and around the ceiling. 'You don't have any CCTV, do you, Mrs Lowerblast?'

The elderly woman shook her head. '*Nein*. I have everything else, but not the video cameras. I never got around to installing them . . . I did not think they were necessarious, with all the other alarms I have here.'

'Hmmm.' He scribbled something down in his notepad, and Phyllis leant closer to see what he was writing.

'And this coat he was wearing. A frock coat, you said?'

'*Ja*. Very old-fashioned. But not shabby. It looked new, in fact, like the tailor had just finished sewing it.'

'Strange,' said Barry Inglis.

'You can say that again,' Phyllis said. 'And don't forget his monocle.'

Barry took a deep breath. 'No, Miss Wong. I have made a note of that.'

'Good. Not many people wear monocles any more.'

Barry said to Mrs Lowerblast, 'Would you mind if I sent in some of the fingerprinting boys? They can take a dusting of both the bookends. Might shed some light.'

'If you think it's a good idea,' Mrs Lowerblast answered. Then she suddenly raised her hand to her mouth and her face went pale. 'Ach! Oh, *nein*!'

'What is it, Mrs L.?'

The Chief Inspector raised an eyebrow.

'Oh,' Mrs Lowerblast said. 'I have just recalled something. Something that had completely escaped from my memory. Until now. You mentioning the fingerprinting boys just brought it back!'

'What, Mrs L.?'

Mrs Lowerblast took out her lavender handkerchief and dotted it across her neck. 'Well, the man in the frock coat, whenever he was here in my shop, *he was wearing gloves*!'

'Oh,' said the Inspector in a sinking tone.

'*Ja*, grey cotton gloves. Oh, how could that have slipped my mind? He never took them off when he was in here. Always they were on his hands.'

'Well, that counts out the fingerprints,' Phyllis said.

The Chief Inspector scribbled in his notepad.

Then he looked up and said, 'Mrs L., I believe that you *do* have a genuine blue wren bookend and a fake one. My problem is, how did you get them? When you originally bought the pair in France, are you sure they were both genuine? I ask you this because I can't for the life of me see how one of them could've been simply swapped like this. Not going on the account you've given me this morning.'

'Of *course* she bought two real ones,' Phyllis said. 'She knows what she bought!'

'Now, now, Miss Wong, I'm only enquiring. I have to ask all sorts of questions to eliminate all possibilities.'

'*Ja*, Chief Inspector,' said Mrs Lowerblast, sadly. 'I have no doubt about what I bought. And I wish you had no doubt about me.'

Outside the shop a few minutes later, the Inspector said, 'I didn't mean to upset her. I was just trying to make some sense of this peculiar business.'

'She's not upset with you,' said Phyllis. 'It's just a terrible thing, and she's a bit rattled by it all.'

Daisy pawed at Phyllis's leg, tapping her lightly near her knee. Phyllis swept the little terrier up and cradled her in her arms like a small furry muff.

'You know,' said the Inspector, 'it could be a case of her memory playing tricks. She purchased the bookends a while ago. Maybe she thinks the pieces she bought are different from what she's got now. It happens. Memory can play strange tricks on people.'

'I believe her,' Phyllis said.

Barry Inglis put his notepad and pen into his pocket and rubbed his thumb across his chin. 'There's something else I don't get. If there *was* a theft . . . or a substitution . . . why would the perpetrator go to all that trouble? Why wouldn't he just go in and grab it, plain and simple? It wouldn't have been hard to get away from Mrs Lowerblast . . . I doubt she's been in training for the city marathon lately.'

Phyllis considered this point.

'And why just take the *one*? Why not both of them? That's where the value lies, in the pair. I mean,' the Inspector said, 'why go through all this . . . this *subterfuge*? It baffles the pants off me, I have to say.' He looked at his watch. 'Oh, good lord, I should've been at the station half an hour ago. Please excuse me won't you, Miss Wong?'

'Sure, Chief Inspector. Thanks for talking to her.'

'Anything for you, Miss Wong. All in the line of duty. Go carefully now.'

And with a tiny raising of the corners of his mouth and a nod, he was off up the sidewalk.

Phyllis stroked the top of Daisy's head. 'I think I need to get Clement over here,' she said to her pup. 'I've got an idea . . .'

❃

Clement was only too glad to meet Phyllis and Daisy. He found them outside The Délicieux Café half an hour later.

Phyllis was watching the street. She'd ducked upstairs and fetched the plushly lined bag in which Daisy would sit happily for hours on end, slung across Phyllis's shoulder. Clement patted the little dog through the bag's straps and Daisy gave his hand a quick and dainty lick.

'I'm glad you called,' Clement said, wiping his hand on his shirt. 'Mum just told me she's entered me into the xylophone eisteddfod next month. Argh! Do you know how much practice I'll have to do? Oh, man . . .'

'Did you bring your webPad?' Phyllis asked.

'Like you asked. Why do you want it?'

'I need you to take some notes.'

'What for?'

'We're going to interview Mrs L. to get her to remember everything about the bookends incident, and you're going to type it all up as she tells us.'

'Why can't *you* type it all up?'

'You're a faster typist than I am.'

Clement blushed proudly. It was true; all those hours spent with his gadgets and his games had given him a certain nimbleness that Phyllis did not possess.

'My fingers are good for sleight of hand, but yours are better for typing. I think,' Phyllis went on, 'it's important we get a record of all that happened. This morning I took Chief Inspector Inglis in there and you know what, Clem? Mrs L. remembered something she'd completely forgotten about the frock-coat guy!'

'What was that?' Clement took off his glasses and began cleaning the lenses with the bottom of his shirt.

'That he was wearing gloves whenever he came in. See, that's why I need to get everything down. If she could forget a fact like that, there might be other things that have slipped her mind as well. Other bits of info might come to light if we can make a proper, step-by-step, point-by-point account with her. And then later you can print it out for me and I can go over it.'

'And over it and over it and over it,' said Clement. 'Knowing you.'

'I want to find out how all of this could've happened.' Phyllis's eyes were bright and urgent. 'I want to pinpoint the exact moment he substituted that bookend. And how he did it.'

'You should have your own TV show. "Getting to the BOTTOM of things, with your host, Phyllis Wong!"' Clement gave a smirk—he always smirked when he could say bottom—and popped his glasses back on.

Phyllis just looked at him. 'You're not taking this very seriously, are you?'

'I'm here, aren't I? Hey, wait for me!' He hurried after her and Daisy as they disappeared through the coloured glass doors of Lowerblast's Antiques & Collectables Emporium.

'But, Phyllis, my dear girl, these things I have just told to Inspector Inglis. You know that. You were here. So close to his elbow I thought you were an extra arm for him . . .'

'Please, Mrs L. Just go over everything one more time. Clem will take everything down. He's very quick. Then we'll go away and I won't bother you again about it.'

'Ach, you are never a botheration.' Mrs Lowerblast sighed and looked at the genuine blue wren bookend in the display case next to her. (She had moved the fake one to the storage area at the back of the shop.) 'Oh, very well. It cannot do any harm, and it is not as though I am being swamped by customers this morning, is it?'

An hour later, after Mrs Lowerblast had been questioned and re-questioned and queried and encouraged to search every corner of her memory by a very thorough Phyllis, and after Clement had typed up every word, barely making any mistakes and applying himself enthusiastically to the task (it sure beat practising the xylophone), Phyllis, Clement and Daisy left Mrs Lowerblast and started walking the four blocks to Clement's apartment building.

They passed all the familiar stores with all their familiar signs and hoardings. Whenever Phyllis and Clement came upon a sign that seemed out-of-place or slightly dumb, they would sometimes play a game. They would speak the words on the sign out loud, in the style in which they were written, or in a voice that conjured up a mood in their heads.

This morning, as the sunshine cast a golden, end-of-summer light across the stores' facades, Phyllis saw a new sign hanging above a narrow doorway. This sign was painted in very bold, black capital letters, and Phyllis couldn't help feeling that it was an order, rather than an invitation.

She stopped in front of the doorway and declared, like a sergeant-major on drill parade: '"**LEARN TO DANCE!**"'

Clement stopped walking, looked at her, then at the sign, then he gave her a short, sharp salute. Anything to avoid being court-martialled. And then he did a smart, swift tap-dance on the spot.

Daisy watched him with a strange expression on her face.

Up ahead was one of their favourites, and now it was Clement's turn.

'"*Madame Stephanie's Face of Hair*",' he read in a growly sort of voice, out the front of the hairdressing salon. He quickly crouched down on the sidewalk, put his fingers on the ground in front of him, raised his head to the shop's awning and went, 'Aaaaaaroooooooohhhhhh!' in the best lycanthropic howl he could manage.

And Daisy did what she always did when he acted like this: she yapped happily and ran all around him, jumping up at his shoulders and getting Phyllis all tangled up in the leash . . .

They were so engrossed in their game that they did not notice the man who had been following them since they had left Mrs Lowerblast's.

The man who had furtively tailed them on the shadowy sides of the streets.

The man who had earlier heard every word spoken in the antiques store, thanks to a listening device he had secretly adhered to the underside of Mrs Lowerblast's counter.

The man who, even in this warm weather, was wearing a highly unusual coat and an even more unusual eyepiece . . .

A fine-toothed comb

That night after dinner Phyllis sprawled across her bed with all the pages Clement had printed scattered across her doona. Daisy was lying at the bottom of the bed, half-asleep, her ears cocked and ever-alert.

Clement had typed up, in point form, all that Mrs Lowerblast had told them. Now Phyllis was reading through the points, numbering each one and trying to find any pattern that might begin to emerge about the behaviour of the man in the frock coat.

When she reached the end of the list, she had numbered over forty different facts. She pulled out a yellow notepad and a pen. Then she thought for a few minutes, before writing the heading:

What did he do with the bookends when he was in the shop?

She began going through the notes. Whenever she found that one of them related directly to what the man had done with the bookends while he was in Mrs Lowerblast's emporium, Phyllis would write that particular point down in her pad, with its corresponding number in front of it.

Soon she had written down all the relevant points. She took a coin from her pocket and, as she read through her new list in the notepad, she manipulated the coin absent-mindedly back and forth across the backs of all of her long, slender fingers, without once touching it with her fingertips. (Her father had taught her how to do this; he had learnt it from his father, who had learnt it from Wallace Wong. It was a great way to keep the fingers in shape for sleight of hand.)

Phyllis's eyes narrowed as she read:

12. He asked to see the bookends.
14. He didn't touch them on his first visit.
16. On the second visit he asked if he could hold them. Mrs L. let him. He picked up one, then he put it down. Then he picked up the other.
18. On the second visit, when he was holding each bookend, he stretched his middle finger and thumb apart and held them against the base of each of the bookends.

Here, Phyllis bit her bottom lip. She re-read point 18. She put down the coin. Then she wrote in the margin next to it: *was he measuring them?*

She continued reading through the points.

24. Third visit: he asked if he could take photos of the bookends to see if they would go with other things in his collection at home.
25. Mrs L. agrees and gets them out for him. Puts them on the display mat on counter.
26. He moved them around, arranging them for the photo.
27. Mrs L. never took her eyes off him or the bookends.
29. He took the photo and left, saying he'd be back in a couple of days to let Mrs L. know if he was going to buy or not.
30. The bookends were in *exactly* the same place they'd been before he took the photo.

Phyllis flipped over a page in her notepad. Quickly she wrote: *He measured them with his hand. He took the photos so that he'd have a visual record of the bookend to help him make the fake as realistic as possible.*

She sat back and read what she'd just written. Somewhere inside her she felt that maybe she'd hit on something. Maybe she was starting to get somewhere . . .

She turned to a new page and made another heading:

What details stand out about frock-coat guy's appearance?

Now she went back through the original list and began to pull out all the facts relating to this. These she wrote down, with their corresponding numbers next to them.

3. He wore a dark blue frock coat with velvet collar.
4. He wore gloves.

(This time, with Phyllis and Clement, Mrs Lowerblast had remembered that detail early on.)

5. He wore a monocle in his right eye.
6. He was tall and thin.
7. Not very old.
8. Punched face.

Phyllis frowned. Then she quickly corrected Clement's error.

8. Pinched face.

9. Long dark hair combed back, shoulder-length.
10. Potty lips.

Phyllis rolled her eyes. She made another correction.

10. Pouty lips.
11. Had a scar running diagonally from his right eye to halfway down his cheek, reddish-brown.
17. His hands were like a pianist's—long fingers, delicate.
38. The last time Mrs L. saw him, his eyes were glowing bright green!!!!!!!!!!!!!!!!!!!!!!!!!!!!!!

(All the exclamation marks were Clement's contribution. Even though Mrs Lowerblast had told them that fact with some amazement, Clement had thought that a little extra emphasis would be helpful.)

Phyllis shuddered slightly. The glowing eyes *was* a weird detail, truly weird.

There was something else Phyllis needed to get into some sort of order. On a new page, she wrote a third heading:

What about his bag?

Once again, she pulled out the relevant facts and listed them:

19. Black leather.
20. Tallish, oblong-shaped, with handle at the top.
21. Like a high, thin briefcase.
22. Every time he came in, he put it on the counter to his left.
23. He never opened it on any of his visits.
28. He moved the bag off the counter before he photographed the bookends, putting it on the floor.

Phyllis sighed. She went back to the original list that Clement had printed out and quickly looked through it. The other facts recorded there were mostly about Gladys Reyscombe—a few bits and pieces that Mrs Lowerblast had told them about the potter and her blue wren bookends. Background information, Phyllis decided.

For half an hour, Phyllis sat there, cross-legged, re-reading all her notes. She did something she always did whenever she concentrated intensely: she raised her little finger on her left hand and the thumb on her right hand. Then, while she was absorbed, she brought her hands together and intertwined her little finger and her thumb, and she wrapped the rest of her fingers around the backs of her hands.

She sat like this, totally still and breathing softly, as if she were almost a statue, or time itself had somehow been suspended, unmoving, around her.

Then she unlocked her hands, straightened her legs and lay back, resting her head on one of her pillows. She stared up at the high ceiling of her bedroom. 'We've got to work out *how* this was done, Daisy.'

Daisy raised her snout, opened one eye and made a small *rrrrrr*-ing sound.

'If we can't work that out, why, people will think that Mrs L. is wrong—that she's always had a real bookend and a fake. And if frock-coat guy is found, and brought to trial, well, the case won't stick unless we can prove how he could have pulled it off!'

The mini foxy put her head down again—she had tigers to chase in her dreams, and she knew she could catch them tonight.

Phyllis let her eyes wander across the ceiling, taking in all the ornate plaster mouldings of stars and obelisks and palm trees and tiny top hats and sunrises that sat jauntily around the cornices. She loved the ceiling in her room; she could look at the patterns and the shapes for hours on end and let her mind wander to faraway places or times from the past.

Slowly, like water draining away after a warm, pleasant bath, a thought pulled at Phyllis. A dreadful feeling.

She suspected, deep in her heart, what was going to happen next.

She sat bolt upright, and the colour left her face.

Daisy sprang up, sensing the alarm that had swept over her friend. She rushed across the bed and leapt into Phyllis's lap.

'Daisy! Oh, no! *He's going to come back for the other one!*'

Back-to-base

It was nearly two days before Phyllis managed to track down Chief Inspector Barry Inglis again.

She'd tried knocking on his door the next morning, but he had already left for duty. Either that or he was working the night shift. Phyllis knew he alternated between days and nights, depending on what crimes were going down or what task-forces were in operation. So she took Daisy for a walk to the station to find out where he was.

When they arrived the policewoman at the front desk told Phyllis the Chief Inspector was away on a case and wouldn't be back until later.

'When?' Phyllis asked.

'I can't tell you that,' the policewoman answered, peering at her computer screen (as if that would make Phyllis suddenly disappear).

'But I need to know. It's important.'

'Is it a police matter?' asked the policewoman, not looking at Phyllis.

Phyllis frowned. 'Well . . . it is. It should be. I mean, I think it will be, before we know it . . .'

The policewoman was typing now on her keypad. 'Then maybe you'd like to see one of the constables on duty?'

'No, I need to see Barry. I mean, Chief Inspector Inglis. I know him, you see. Personally.'

'And what's your name?'

'Phyllis. Phyllis Wong. He knows about what I'm going to tell him. He knows the case already.'

At this, the policewoman stopped typing and looked at Phyllis. 'The case?' she questioned, one eye half closing.

Phyllis twisted the end of Daisy's leash around her fingers. 'Well, it's not a case. Not yet. But it will be. I know it will be. And he knows the lady involved; he lives in the same building.'

Now the policewoman leant forward. 'He knows the lady involved, eh?' she repeated. 'Now why doesn't *that* surprise me?'

Phyllis didn't know if the policewoman wanted her to answer the question or not, and she didn't really understand why the policewoman had asked her that. She bit her lip. 'I don't know. Maybe you don't surprise easily?'

Then something mildly astonishing happened: the policewoman smiled, and it was as if she had been replaced by an identical policewoman, but with a more friendly nature. 'Okay then, Phyllis Wong,' she said, giving Phyllis a wink. 'Let's find out when your friend Chief Inspector Inglis gets back.'

'Thanks,' said Phyllis, a little stunned at the instantaneous transformation.

The policewoman typed and then checked the computer screen. 'Ah. He's due back in here tomorrow morning.'

'Thanks. What time?'

'When we see him.' The policewoman raised one eyebrow. 'He's usually in by 9:30.'

'Peachy. I'll head him off at the pass.'

'Pardon?' said the policewoman.

'Um . . . nothing. Thank you very much; I appreciate your help. Bye now. C'mon, Daisy.'

Daisy gave a soft yap and Phyllis started to leave.

'You're welcome,' said the policewoman. 'Oh! Did he tell you he's just been promoted?'

'No,' said Phyllis, turning. 'What's he now?'

'Oh, he's still Barry Inglis,' the policewoman said, smiling. 'I mean, he's still a Chief Inspector. But as of next month he'll be heading the Fine Arts and Antiques Squad.'

'Wow!' Phyllis gave her a puzzled look. 'I never knew Barry was into fine arts and antiques . . .'

'The man is full of surprises,' said the policewoman. 'Or so it seems.'

❃

For the rest of that day, Phyllis and Daisy stayed close to Mrs Lowerblast's emporium. Occasionally they went in and talked to Mrs Lowerblast; the rest of the time they sat on the front steps of the Wallace Wong Building, Phyllis pretending to read the latest issue of *Legerdemain* magazine (one of several magazines about magic her father had subscribed to for her). She was always keeping an eye on the front door of Mrs Lowerblast's store.

Clement texted in the afternoon, trying to get out of xylophone practice by asking her what she was doing. Phyllis replied, with one word: *stakeout*.

Clement came over straightaway.

'So,' he said, plonking himself on the steps beside her and Daisy. 'You're just going to sit here all day?'

'Mm-hm. Just keeping watch until I can get the Chief Inspector to do something.'

'Which will be . . .?'

'I'll nab him first thing in the morning. He always has breakfast at the Délicieux.'

Daisy licked the back of Clement's hand and

then his fingers—she had detected traces of peanut butter, and she wasn't about to lose the scent.

'Hey, cut it out, Deebs!' Clement wiped his fingers on his pants, and Daisy started snouting around there instead while Clement got his phone out of his backpack and started linking up to one of the online gaming communities he belonged to. 'Hey, Phyll?'

'What?'

'Do you plan to sit here all night? I mean, what're you gonna do when Mrs L. goes home after five?'

Phyllis watched the people coming and going in front of them. 'I've thought about that,' she said. 'No, I'm not going to stay here all night. The emporium is alarmed so if frock-coat guy tried to break in we'd all hear the alarms go off. Anyway, that's not how he works. If he was just a simple smash-and-grab thief he wouldn't have bothered substituting the first bookend, would he?'

'I guess not,' said Clement, pushing his glasses back up his nose with one hand and frantically pressing the keys on his phone with the other, as he tried to ward off a flank of vampire zombie accountants from the planet Boomdiddy Vostock.

'No,' Phyllis said, cupping her chin in her hands and resting her elbows on her knees. 'He's smarter than that . . . this guy plans things out, and we've got to stay one step in front of him.'

First thing on Wednesday morning, as Chief Inspector Inglis was about to tuck into his breakfast of fried eggs, bacon, French toast, mushrooms, grilled tomatoes, pommes noisettes and coffee, Phyllis burst into The Délicieux Café and sat down in the seat opposite him.

'He's coming back!' she said breathlessly. 'I've gone through all the facts, Chief Inspector, all the details. He's going to come back for the other one!'

Pierre Ravissant hurried across to the table. '*Bonjour*, Phyllees!' he greeted her over his shoulder. 'Zermzeeng zweet fer ze asternishing and breelliant mademoiselle, *oui*?'

'Hi, Pierre. No, not today . . . oh, okay, yes please, thanks.'

'Pascaline!' called Pierre. 'Ze 'ot chocolate and ze *pain au chocolat* for Phyllees, *s'il vous plait*.' Pascaline smiled and waved at Phyllis as Pierre, with a small wriggle of his neat moustache, went back to the kitchen.

Barry Inglis had had a forkful of eggs, bacon and toast halfway to his mouth when Phyllis had appeared like an unstoppable tornado. It was still suspended there as he looked at her across the table. 'Miss Wong,' he greeted her. 'Good morning. What exactly are you referring to?'

'The frock-coat guy! He's going to return and get the other blue wren bookend! Look!'

She pulled all of her notes from her backpack and spread them out on the table for the Inspector to see. He put the forkful of breakfast into his mouth and chewed as he perused all her jottings and the print-outs.

'Hmm,' he said after he'd swallowed. 'You've been busy.'

'We've got to do something to protect Mrs L.,' Phyllis said in a low voice. 'We can't let him get away with this again!'

Barry sighed and piled more eggs and bacon onto his fork. 'He'd be foolish to come back,' he said. 'We have a very good description of him. We know exactly what he looks like.' He shovelled the food into his mouth.

'I've thought about that,' said Phyllis as Pascaline brought her order to the table. 'Thanks, Pascaline.'

'Pleasure, treasure.' She hurried back to the counter to serve a customer.

'We do know what he looks like,' Phyllis went on, as Barry kept eating. 'But he's not your average thief, Inspector. He's up to something . . . unusual.

I wouldn't be surprised, not one bit, if he comes back *in disguise*.'

Barry stopped chewing. He looked at Phyllis and raised his eyebrows.

'What if he makes himself look different? He looks different already—the way he dresses, the clothes he wears. I mean, come on, he wears a monocle, after all! What's to stop him from changing his appearance completely?'

'I think you've been watching a few too many of your great-grandfather's movies lately, haven't you?'

'Chief Inspector Barry Inglis! Don't treat me like I'm stupid!'

Barry shook his head and frowned. 'I apologise. I have never, in all the time I have known you, thought that about you, Miss Wong.'

Phyllis sipped her hot chocolate.

Barry put down his knife and fork. 'All right. Go on.'

'Well, what if he's just biding his time, letting two or three months slip by before he returns? And then when he *does* return, what if Mrs L. doesn't recognise him? He could pull the same swifty all over again and end up with the pair!'

The Chief Inspector regarded her. Then he picked up Phyllis's notes and began reading.

Phyllis watched him as he scanned each page. She noticed a line of concentration creasing his brow. Occasionally a corner of one of his eyebrows lifted, before being slowly lowered again.

Presently, he gave her back the pages. 'All right. You may have something. I do have to say that I'm still not 100 per cent convinced that the bookend *has* been substituted—'

'Are you saying Mrs L. is—?'

'Steady on, Miss Wong. Allow me to finish. But I *am* convinced your theory is not without some basis for further action.'

'So what are you going to do?'

The Inspector had another mouthful of breakfast and thought. 'As soon as I get in to the station, I'll arrange for the security boys to come and visit Mrs Lowerblast and install a back-to-base alarm. Then, if this suspect does return, or if anyone shows any suspicious interest in the blue wren bookends, all she'll have to do is press a small button at the back of the counter. It will send a signal directly to the guys at the station—we have a network of these types of alarms, and there are always officers on alert. That might prevent a scenario like the one you're concerned about.'

'I hope so.'

'I will also,' said Barry, between mouthfuls, 'get the security boys to encourage Mrs Lowerblast to put in closed circuit video cameras. She should've had them installed long ago.'

'Do you think,' Phyllis asked, 'that it'll all be enough?'

'We never know,' Barry answered. 'But it's all we can do.'

Phyllis smiled. 'Thank you, Inspector.'

'You're welcome.'

'And congrats on your promotion!'

'Ah. Fine Arts and Antiques,' he said. 'Can you believe it? I know as much about things like that as I do about doing the tango or breeding poultry. Which is next-to-nothing. How I got that job is beyond me. And there's the wonder of the thing, Miss Wong.'

*

In the afternoon, Phyllis, Clement and Daisy were present as two plain-clothes police officers installed the back-to-base alarm system in Mrs Lowerblast's emporium.

Mrs Lowerblast had been a little taken aback when they arrived, but Phyllis explained what was going on and told her friend not to worry—this was the next best thing to having Chief Inspector Inglis right there with her all the time. Mrs Lowerblast soon settled down and gladly let them carry out their work.

Clement was very intrigued by all the gadgetry, and more than once the officers had to politely ask him to step out of the way while the wiring was being positioned.

Daisy slept in her small patch of kaleidoscopic sunlight near the front windows throughout all of the activity.

Phyllis stood in the corner of the shop and watched. She felt a bit better that the Inspector had organised all of this. But she still felt, deep inside, that things were not yet finished with the mystery of the blue wren bookends.

She had to work out *how* it had been done.

That evening, on the other side of the city, along a sidewalk lit up by garish neon signs that shone in the dark, oily puddles, a tall, thin man was striding.

He moved with his chest puffed out and his head held high. In his hand he swung an ebony walking cane, its silver top clasped tightly in his gloved fist.

The man did not yield the sidewalk to other pedestrians. Rather, he ploughed ahead, brandishing his cane and stopping for no one. He fixed all with a steely, impenetrable gaze.

Thus propelled, he turned a corner into a gloomy alleyway. He clutched his cane so tightly his knuckles were turning white underneath his glove.

The girl, he was thinking. *The tall girl with the fleabag dog and the boy with the glasses. They knew.*

He disappeared into the dimness, his blue frock coat dissolving into the inky night.

They would have

have

have

to be dealt with.

PART TWO

Do you believe in ghosts?

Right under our very noses

Phyllis felt a bit more relaxed knowing that Mrs Lowerblast would be looked after if the worst thing happened.

The warm days were coming to an end by the time school was ready to resume. Phyllis, Daisy and Clement had hung about, going to the movies, having fish and chips in City Park and watching people (Phyllis did that) and playing games on a new handheld gaming console in an attempt to avoid xylophone lessons (Clement did that) and sniffing around bushes, lampposts and mailboxes (neither Phyllis nor Clement engaged in those activities). And whenever Phyllis left her apartment or returned to the Wallace Wong Building, she always called in to say hi to Mrs Lowerblast and to check that all was okay.

And all had been.

Phyllis thought less and less about frock-coat guy as the vacation came to an end. She didn't forget about him, but he faded into a place at the back of her mind, only emerging occasionally when Phyllis saw a stranger in the street wearing an unusual coat or carrying a black bag of curious dimensions.

The leaves began to change colour. The tall row of Japanese crabapples that lined Phyllis's street, and the crepe myrtles that grew on Clement's a few blocks away, were starting to paint the city with their glowing palettes of red and orange and deep, deep yellow.

And the chill winds were creeping in, swirling around the corners of the buildings and gently shaking the colours out of the branches around town.

❃

One afternoon Phyllis and Clement were coming into the Wallace Wong Building on their way home from school when a colourful, glamorous, zhooshy woman burst down the stairs like a perfumed cluster of runaway balloons.

'Phyllis!' Minette Bulbolos gushed. 'Phyllis the fearless! How have you been?'

Phyllis smiled. The sight of Minette Bulbolos, always dressed in her bright, shimmery clothes, never failed to make her feel buoyant and cheerful.

'Hi, Minette. You know my good friend, Clem?'

'I have not met him before this, but—' she fluttered her extra-long eyelashes at him and gave Phyllis a slight wink—'now that I have, my life will be propelled beyond the galaxies! How do you do, Clem?'

'Um . . . um . . . um . . . well, um . . .' Clement had never seen anyone like Minette Bulbolos before.

'Minette lives on the next floor up,' Phyllis told Clement. 'Across the landing from Chief Inspector Inglis.'

'Um . . . I see,' said Clement, his eyes wide behind his glasses.

At the sound of the Chief Inspector's name, Minette gave a sigh. 'Oh, that man. Always coming and going, but never here long enough to accept an invitation to one of my dinners. Ah, well. Perhaps one day I can indulge him . . . He has yet to taste my Turkish Delights.' Her bosom rose and fell, and she fluttered her heavy lashes once more.

'Have you been away?' Phyllis asked.

'Oh, yes, my *habibi*. I was working in Abu Dhabi for a month. They pay very well over there.' She winked again.

'Minette's a belly dancer,' Phyllis said to Clement. 'The best belly dancer you ever saw!'

'Um . . . um . . .' Clement's cheeks and neck had flushed a very deep crimson.

'Have you seen *many* belly dancers, Clem?' Minette asked him.

'Um . . . no, not really,' Clement stammered. 'I don't have much time. I have to . . . practise . . . um . . . the xylophone . . . um . . .'

'And he's always gaming,' said Phyllis.

'Ah!' Minette gave him a wide smile. 'Why shouldn't you? Life, after all, should be one *big* game. Life and love and work . . . which is where I'm off to now. Work. We are rehearsing a new act at the Baubles of Baalbek Nightclub, and I have to become accustomed to my new anaconda. Oh, I hope they have chosen one with a friendly disposition this time. The last one I had to work with used to love wrapping itself around my face whenever I was about to launch into my *zaghareet*!' She sighed in a theatrical manner. 'But sometimes these little things are sent to test us, don't you agree?'

'Um,' said Clement.

Phyllis smiled.

'Until next time,' said Minette, hitching her big velvet bag over her shoulder and giving Clement a little shimmy. 'Goodbye, Phyllis! Goodbye, Mr Xylophones!'

And with a wave of her multi-ringed fingers she wafted out of the lobby.

Phyllis pressed the elevator button. 'What came over you?' she asked Clement.

'What do you mean?'

'You were blushing like global warming!'

The elevator doors opened and Clement dived in. 'It's just hot in here, that's all.'

Phyllis followed him. 'Yeah, sure.' She put her key into the control panel and pressed the button for the top floor.

Clement tried to change the subject. 'Hey, Phyll,' he said, studying the panel. 'Why's the button for the basement always locked?'

The doors closed and the elevator began ascending. 'I don't know.'

'Does your key work it?'

'No. This only lets us go up to my apartment.'

'So who's got the key to the basement?'

'Dad, probably.' Phyllis had sometimes wondered about why that basement button needed a key, but it had never been a *niggling* sort of wonder, and the curiosity about it had never lingered in her mind for long. The Wallace Wong Building was old, after all, and, as with many old buildings, forgotten, deserted places and the shadows of history were often found within . . .

The elevator arrived at her floor and stopped with a loud and jolting shudder.

'*Blerd-erblerd-erblerd-erblerd-erblerd-erblerd-er*!' went Clement, shaking his head as if trying to regain his senses.

'Thank you for sharing that with me,' said Phyllis, laughing—it wasn't the first time he had done that when the elevator had stopped in such a manner. 'C'mon, let's get Daisy and take her walkies.'

Clement pushed his glasses back up his nose. 'Let's get gelato too, yeah?'

'Yes, Mr Xylophones. Whatever you want.'

'Very funny,' said Clement, blushing again at the thought of Minette Bulbolos.

❄

'Do you believe in ghosts, Miss Wong?'

It was Saturday morning and Phyllis had been on her way out to walk Daisy in City Park when she'd spotted Inspector Inglis having coffee and a few donuts while reading his newspaper in The Délicieux Café, and had popped in to say hello.

'Ghosts?' she said, plonking herself down in the chair opposite. Daisy sprang up onto her lap, her snout scouring the table for the promise of any stray delectable crumbs.

'Mmm.' Barry Inglis chewed on a donut. His eyes seemed clouded and a fine crease ran across the centre of his forehead. 'Ghosts,' he said in a low voice. 'Spirits. Phantoms. Invisible forces of . . . *weirdness*.'

Phyllis shook her head. 'I don't think so. I mean, I've never really thought about it. Dad's told me that my grandmother and my great-grandmother used to believe in them, though. Ghost stories are quite common where my family originally came from.'

'Hmmm.' Barry sipped his coffee. 'It seems ghosts might be becoming more common around here, as well.'

Pascaline suddenly appeared at Phyllis's elbow. 'Whert would you like thees merning, Phyllees, *mon cheri*?'

Phyllis smiled and ordered a chocolate milkshake.

'And I will breeng a leetle berl erf water fer mademoiselle Daisy,' said Pascaline, before hurrying off.

Phyllis leant towards the Inspector, pinioning Daisy against the edge of the table. 'What do you mean, becoming more common around here?'

'Aaaah,' he said, shaking his head. 'The guys down at the station think there're ghosts involved. They can't find any other explanation for it.'

'Involved in what?'

'In the heist.'

'What heist?' Phyllis sometimes wished that Chief Inspector Inglis was not a man of such few words.

Barry looked all around the café. Then he spoke in a voice barely louder than a whisper: 'The biggest jewellery robbery this city's seen in fifty years.'

Phyllis said nothing, but widened her eyes to encourage him to go on.

'We're keeping it quiet,' he told her. 'We've kept it right away from the press. Seems the jewellery store involved has to sort out some . . . complications . . . with their insurance company and with the owners of the piece that was stolen. Besides, we'd look like a laughing-stock if we went public with what's happened.' He chomped into a donut and frowned.

'What was taken?' asked Phyllis.

The Inspector put down the donut. He lowered his head so that the lobes of his ears were almost level with his shoulders, and fixed Phyllis with a steady, direct gaze. 'The Van Rockechild diamond necklace!' he announced quietly, his blue eyes shining at her.

'Oh!' gasped Phyllis.

Pascaline brought Phyllis's milkshake and a

bowl of water. 'Enjoy, Phyllees!' And off she went to serve some other customers.

Daisy jumped down from Phyllis's lap and had a drink from the water bowl, her pink tongue lapping at the water. Then she turned around three times and became a small furry ball, settling at Phyllis's feet.

'You've heard of it, then?' asked Barry.

'I sure have.' Phyllis's father had told her about the Van Rockechild diamond necklace when it had been announced in the newspapers several months ago that the priceless piece would be on display in the window of Duckworth's (the city's most exclusive jewellery store) for a short time. Phyllis's dad had taken a special interest in the news, not because he was dazzled by the brilliance of the necklace—though it had no fewer than one hundred and forty-five large, flawless 20-carat pink, blue and white diamonds studding a gold and platinum chain—but because he was involved in the insurance industry. He had said to Phyllis at the time, 'That's one account I'm glad we *don't* have, Phyll—imagine the payout if it was nabbed!'

'Yeah,' Barry said. 'It's one of the most valuable pieces of bling in the world. Been owned by maharajahs and princesses. And the odd punter who got lucky with his money along the line. It's got what we in the business call a chequered history.'

'When was it stolen?'

'Two nights ago.'

'How?' Phyllis slurped her milkshake.

Barry shook his head and leant back in his seat. 'It just . . . *disappeared.*'

Phyllis stopped slurping. 'What?'

'From right under our noses. It just disappeared. One moment it was there, the next—vanished!'

'That's impossible!'

'Yeah. That's right. Impossible. But, Miss Wong, for the first time in my career, the impossible has happened.'

'But how do you know it just disappeared?'

'Ah, now there's the wonder of the thing: we've got it all on film!'

Phyllis gasped. 'What?'

'We've got the security footage. We can see all that happened, and when it happened, and . . .' He trailed off and looked at her, his head cocked slightly to one side.

'What's up, Chief Inspector?'

Barry Inglis scrutinised his young friend. This case was totally flummoxing him; he had never seen the like of it before. Things disappearing into thin air! A thought went through his mind and, in true detective style, he pushed it around in there, rolling it over and over, tossing it up and catching it again, batting it back and forth as though it were a ball in the tennis court of his brain. Then, still looking at Phyllis, he nodded his head slowly and the corners of his lips rose slightly. *What did he have to lose, after all? She did have a good way of thinking . . .*

'Chief Inspector! Helloooo?'

He blinked at her, and was back at the table again. 'Oh, pardon me. Miss Wong, I've just had an idea. I really shouldn't be doing this, but . . . I'd like you to see exactly what I mean. Would you care to view the footage?'

'Would I? You bet! When? Can we go now?' Phyllis was nearly halfway out of her seat.

'No, not today. Too many people about headquarters on Saturdays. I tell you what, though, how about we meet here tomorrow morning at 0830 hours? We can call in to the station before my tennis game. It won't take long.'

'Swell,' said Phyllis, beaming. One of the best things about Chief Inspector Inglis was that he always treated her like she was worthwhile.

'Good,' said Barry. 'Prepare to be amazed.'

'Can't wait. And don't worry, Chief Inspector, I'll keep it under wraps.'

The corners of Barry Inglis's lips curled a little more as he went back to reading his newspaper and finishing his donuts.

Phyllis slurped the rest of her milkshake. She picked up Daisy's leash and stood to go. Then she stopped. 'Chief Inspector?'

'Mmm?' He peered up from his paper.

'Why are you letting me see the footage?'

'Well, to be honest with you, Miss Wong, I need all the ideas I can get at this point. And ideas,' he added with a sigh, 'are things that you seem to have plenty of.'

The disappearance

Next morning, the Inspector met Phyllis sharply at 0830 hours and took her to headquarters. He got her past the front desk and up in the elevator to his office without any fuss.

'Have a seat,' he said, gesturing to one of two chairs in front of his desk.

'Cool office, Chief Inspector.' Phyllis had never set foot past the front desk of the building before. 'Great view.' She looked out across the vista of City Park, with the Metropolitan Art Gallery in the distance and the rows of gleaming skyscrapers lining the perimeter of the park below.

'Mmm. I've only just moved in here. It came with the Fine Arts and Antiques promotion. Not that I've got a lot of time to gaze out of the window, Miss Wong. Not when I have cases like this one.' He was fiddling with the cables at the back of a TV on his desk.

'Hey, I can see the roof terrace of our building!'

'Yes,' Barry said, frowning as he took a cable out of one socket and put it into another. 'That's the first thing I looked for when I moved in here. I like to know I can see home if there's a fire or something.'

'Or if you get homesick,' said Phyllis.

'Yes, although I can't say that happens very often to me. Now, Miss Wong, please sit down. We don't have a lot of time, you know.'

Phyllis smiled and sat in one of the chairs.

'Right,' said Barry, picking up the remote. 'This should be cued at around about the right spot . . . let's see . . .'

He pressed the play button and the screen flickered to life.

'Okay, this is the scene viewed through the front window of Duckworth's. The cameras are positioned on the outside of the window, attached to the sidewalk awning in a recessed alcove near the ceiling. The glass in the window is bomb-proof security tensile, by the way, not that that has any bearing on what's about to happen.'

In the top right-hand corner of the screen, a small timer was ticking over, second by second, and Phyllis kept one eye on this and one eye on the rest of the scene.

'There, Miss Wong, you can see the display

stand in the centre of the window.' Barry zoomed in to the centre of the frame. 'And there, on the middle of the stand, is the Van Rockechild diamond necklace.'

Phyllis gasped. The necklace was sitting on a deep blue velvet platform, lit by a dozen bright halogen downlights. The facets of each of the one hundred and forty-five pink, blue and white diamonds sparkled and dazzled brilliantly.

To Phyllis, they were like a cluster of the brightest galaxies all suspended in a time-locked, miniature universe.

'What you can't see,' the Inspector continued, zooming out again to display the whole scene in the window, 'is that there is a bullet-proof glass cube over the necklace. It's so clean—no fingerprints or marks or anything—that it's not visible to the naked eye. The glass cube is sitting on the display stand, effectively sealing the Van Rockechild necklace in its own little chamber.'

Phyllis looked very hard, but Barry was right; she could not see any trace of the glass cube.

'Now,' Barry said, looking at the ticking time display, 'watch carefully. In fifteen seconds . . . keep your eye on the necklace . . .'

Phyllis bit her lip. She focussed hard on the Van Rockechild diamond necklace, so hard that she almost stopped breathing.

Ten . . .

Five . . .

Two . . .

One . . .

. . . *and it was gone!*

She shook her head quickly back and forth. Her jaw dropped open. She looked at Barry, then at the screen, then at the Chief Inspector again. 'But . . . but . . .' was all she could stammer.

Barry nodded. 'It's not often I see *you* speechless. Disappeared into thin air, like I said!'

'It can't have,' Phyllis said. 'It was right there. It was there, and then . . . it *wasn't*!'

'You can see why some of the guys think there're ghosts involved, can't you?'

'Play it again, Inspector?'

'Certainly, Miss Wong.' He rewound the tape and replayed the scene.

Phyllis watched carefully. Once again, the Van Rockechild necklace was sitting in all its shining glory on the display stand and then, in a nano-instant, the display stand was completely empty.

'And again?' Phyllis asked. 'Can you do it frame-by-frame this time?'

'That I can.' He replayed the footage one frame at a time.

She watched like a hawk. She focussed hard on

the necklace, concentrating on its shape on the dark blue velvet stand. The dazzling diamonds filled her eyes . . . second by second . . . moment . . . by . . . moment . . .

. . . then, nothing!

It had vanished into thin air!

'I know!' Phyllis said, slapping the arm of the chair. 'There's a trap-door in the stand. There's a trap-door and a descending little platform that dropped quickly down, quicker than a blink, and the trap-door sprang straight back into place. It's sometimes used in magic for an instantaneous vanish!'

Barry shook his head. 'That could have been a possibility,' he said, 'but we screened off the area and the forensics people pulled the stand apart. No gimmickry at all. And anyway, on the rest of the footage there's no sign of anyone going anywhere near the stand.'

Phyllis intertwined her thumb and little finger, bringing her hands together. 'Hmmm. Chief Inspector?'

'Yes?'

'Have any frames been cut out of this film? Has anyone tinkered with it and edited it since the heist?'

'No,' he answered emphatically. 'I can assure you they have not. The CCTV footage was taken straightaway by the force and a copy was made of the whole tape. That copy is in the vaults downstairs, and the film experts here have compared both copies. Both of them are identical, with no evidence of any missing footage.' He nodded at her. 'But good thinking, all the same.'

'Were any alarms set off?'

The Inspector shook his head. 'The whole window area has a top-of-the-range alarm system installed, but nothing was triggered off at all. If anyone had entered or left the window display area, we would've heard the sirens.'

'This is screwy,' said Phyllis.

'For want of a better word, it is,' Barry agreed. He switched off the monitor.

'I can see why you want to keep it under wraps, all right.'

Barry was unplugging the screen, and getting a bit discombobulated with all the cables. 'Mmm. Can you imagine the headlines?'

'Hey, Chief Inspector?'

'Yes?'

'Is the window at Duckworth's still set up for the necklace display?'

'I do believe it is,' he answered, holding a bundle

of red, yellow and green cables and looking at them as though they were aliens from outer space. 'The store's put up a sign saying that due to unforeseen circumstances the famous Van Rockechild necklace is no longer on display. We've instructed them not to move anything from the window until tomorrow. We've got an expert from upstate coming to have a last look at the scene, and she can't be with us until tomorrow afternoon. For all intents and purposes it's still a crime scene.'

'Okay,' said Phyllis thoughtfully.

'Thank you for your time this morning,' Barry said, throwing the cables into the corner. 'Now, I must go and slaughter my opponent.'

'Thank *you*,' said Phyllis.

At the front desk on their way out they came across the same policewoman Phyllis had met when she had been trying to track down the Chief Inspector about Mrs Lowerblast's predicament.

The policewoman looked up from her computer as they passed. 'Well, Barry Inglis, all dressed in white,' she said with a sideways smile.

'Good morning, Constable Olofsson,' said Barry, trying to make a quick exit in his tennis clothes.

'And hello to you,' said Constable Olofsson to Phyllis.

'This,' Barry said to the constable, 'is my young colleague, Phyllis Wong.'

'Hello again,' said Phyllis, and Barry looked puzzled.

'We've met,' said Constable Olofsson. 'Been helping out with a case, have we?' she asked Phyllis.

The Inspector frowned. It wasn't really by the book to have civilians in at headquarters, unless they were under investigation or about to be charged. 'Miss Wong has been assisting me. She has a background in . . . mysterious things. She is a first-rate conjuror.'

'Really?' said Constable Olofsson with a smile.

'Watch this,' said Phyllis. She opened both of her hands and waved them through the air to show they were empty. Then she clasped them in front of her and gave Constable Olofsson and Barry Inglis a smile—the same smile that she had inherited from Wallace Wong, Conjuror of Wonder!

Constable Olofsson looked at Barry. He gave her a nod, as if to say *you ain't seen nothin' yet, Constable Olofsson.*

Phyllis made her left hand into a ball. From a pocket in her coat she took out a small, bright green silk handkerchief with her right hand. She shook the silk, letting it unfold and flutter in her fingers. Then she proceeded to stuff it gently into her closed left fist, pushing it in bit by bit with her first finger and then finally stuffing the last of the silk in with her middle finger.

And then, with her great-grandfather's smile and a small theatrical flourish, she took her right hand away and opened her left fist. The green silk had vanished!

'Whoa!' said Constable Olofsson.

Barry's eyebrows shot up—he hadn't seen this one before.

Phyllis displayed both her hands, front and back. There was no sign of the silk anywhere.

'As you can see,' Barry said to the constable, 'my young friend is an expert when it comes to disappearances.'

At the scene

While Barry Inglis went off to slaughter his opponent, Phyllis returned to her apartment and collected Daisy. Together they walked the nine blocks downtown to Duckworth's. (It was a slow and sniffy walk—there had been a light rainfall overnight so for Daisy the city was now a smorgasbord of fresh aromas.)

Being early on a Sunday morning, the jewellery store was yet to open, but that didn't matter to Phyllis: she could see what she wanted to see perfectly well through the window.

The main window was tall and wide with a copper trim all around it. Behind the window was a display area the size of a small room. Phyllis squinted through the glass—it must have been at least half an inch thick.

As the Chief Inspector had said, a sign had been placed on the empty display stand, underneath the glass cube. Today the cube was clearly visible;

the fingerprint people had dusted it thoroughly, and instead of it being totally transparent, it now had a cloudy sheen to it from the fingerprinting powder.

Phyllis slung her backpack onto the sidewalk and took out her phone. She took a quick photo of the sign on the stand:

> We regret to advise that due to circumstances beyond our control the famous Van Rockechild diamond necklace is no longer on display at Duckworth's.

The entire back wall of the display area was shrouded in what appeared to be a ceiling-to-floor drape of deep, dark blue.

Phyllis put her face closer to the window and peered carefully, using her arm and hand to shield the reflection from the glass.

She observed the plush blue velvet curtain. It was so rich in texture and colour that it was almost black. 'I'd say that's some expensive velvet, Daisy,' she muttered, more to herself than to the terrier.

Daisy, who had been sniffing the place where the marble storefront met the pavement, looked up, blinked, and went back to her sniffing.

Phyllis noticed that the same dark blue velvet had been used to cover the display stand, as well as to carpet the floor in the window area.

She stepped back, picking up her bag and hitching it over her shoulder. She pulled Daisy away from the window and took in the scene from this new angle. Apart from all the blue velvet and the display stand and the glass cube and the sign, there was nothing else to be seen.

She took one more shot of the whole window with her phone camera. Then she squinted hard at all that was in front of her. But her mind was emptier than the place where the Van Rockechild necklace had once been on display.

'Why are you in such a hurry?' asked Clement, trying to keep up with Phyllis as she barrelled down the sidewalk on their way home from school the next day.

'You'll see,' she said, darting around a large businessman who had his phone stuck to his ear and who wasn't watching where he was going.

'Hey, this isn't the way home.'

'Taking a slight detour.'

'Where to?' Clement bumped into a woman carrying a wad of files and papers. She flailed her arms all around, like a distressed bird flapping its wings, as she tried to stop the files hurtling out of her grasp. 'Sorry,' Clement said, hurrying on. 'Hey, Phyll, how far are we going?'

'You don't have to come, you know.' Phyllis arrived at a set of lights and banged the pedestrian button four times.

Clem caught up with her while she waited to cross. He tucked his shirt in, swivelling his backpack out of the way and causing his laptop to almost fall out of the unzipped opening. 'Whoops,' he said, catching it at the last minute. 'Mum'd kill me if I broke this one.'

'It's not as if you have far to go to replace it,' Phyllis said. 'It's not every kid whose parents own the biggest appliance store in town.' The lights changed and she started powering across the street.

'Yeah, but it'd be the third one this year. Plus the iPod I dropped down the toilet. And the phone I lost on the excursion to the Science Museum. Mum says I have to *pay* for the next one.' He shuddered at the thought of that, even if he *would* be paying wholesale price.

'Oh,' he said, 'while I think of it, do you and your dad want a new juicer? Mum's got too many in the store and she can't send them back and they're really good, even with carrots. That's what the salespeople always say to customers . . . it's the thing about being good with carrots that sells more juicers than anything else you can tell them, and—'

'Yes, Clem, thank you for sharing all that with me,' smiled Phyllis, which is what she always said whenever Clement went on about appliances or gizmos.

She turned left into one of the bigger avenues where many high-end stores were located. She saw the Duckworth's storefront and smiled. 'Let's hope she's still there . . .' she muttered.

Clement pushed his glasses further up his nose and hurried along with her. 'Who's still there? Who's still *where*?'

Phyllis all but ran the last few steps to the window. She leant on the glass and put her hands above her forehead so she could peer inside. 'That must be her,' she said quietly.

Clement squinted through the window. Inside the display area he saw a tall, large-shouldered woman with severely cropped bright reddish-pinkish hair. She was wearing narrow, oblong-shaped, blue-rimmed glasses and was scowling and stabbing with her finger at the keys on a Blackberry, which she clutched in her claw-like hand.

Phyllis couldn't help thinking that she looked like a dragon in a business suit.

'Who's that?' Clement asked.

'That's the expert,' Phyllis answered. She bit her lip as she kept watching. She was hoping for something . . . hoping for *someone* to be here as well . . .

'Expert in what?'

'I can't tell you,' Phyllis said. 'It's—*yes*!'

The dark blue drapes at the back of the display area had been pulled swiftly aside, and Chief Inspector Inglis had appeared, looking a little flustered.

'Hey,' Clement said. 'It's the Chief Inspector!'

Barry Inglis went up to dragon-woman and said a few words. The woman stopped stabbing at her Blackberry and gave him a look of such withering-ness that Barry almost took a step back from her.

'What's happening?' asked Clement.

Phyllis kept her eye on what was going on in the window. 'Clem, I can't tell you. The Chief said it all has to be kept under wraps.'

'Huh?' said Clement, his voice small. As far as he knew, except for how she did her magic, Phyllis Wong had never kept any secrets from him.

'I'm going to see if I can get in there,' she said urgently. 'I want to sniff out a few things.' She turned to her friend. 'I'm sorry, Clem, but I have to go in alone.'

'Really?' His voice was smaller. He took a deep breath and adjusted his glasses. 'Ha.' He smiled, weakly. 'The way you're talking, you sound like you're going into a war zone!'

Phyllis smiled back at him and gave him a gentle punch on his arm. 'No, it's just Duckworth's. There're no zombie vampire accountants in there.'

Clement shrugged. 'Oh, well. I guess I should go home and do my practice. I'm being forced to learn *The Ride of the Valkyries*. Do you have any idea how hard that is to do on the xylophone? My wrists feel like they're gonna explode!' He sighed. 'See you tomorrow at school, yeah?'

'You bet. Skype me later if you want.'

'Yeah, whatever.' He hitched up his backpack and turned to dawdle home.

'Clem?'

He turned back. 'Yeah?'

'Thanks.'

He gave her a big grin and two thumbs-up. Then off he went.

Phyllis watched him leave. When he'd gone around the corner she turned back to the window. Barry was still there with the dragon-lady, who appeared to be talking very forcefully to him. Or *at* him, Phyllis thought.

She took a deep breath and banged loudly on the window.

The dragon-lady's head shot around, her narrow-framed eyes fixing on Phyllis. The Chief Inspector saw her too and while he didn't smile, his shoulders relaxed and he seemed to cringe less. He raised his hand at his young friend.

Dragon-lady saw him do this. She asked him something as she looked at Phyllis.

He replied.

Phyllis mimed the words, 'Can I come in?' through the glass.

Barry Inglis pulled the sort of face he would have pulled if someone had just poured a bucket of ice down his pants.

That was good enough for Phyllis—he hadn't shaken his head or said no or anything. She smiled at him and then hurried round to the front doors of the store.

A big doorman wearing a burgundy-coloured double-breasted uniform with shiny gold buttons and a peaked cap was standing by the doors, ready to open them to any customer who, in his opinion, would be welcome in the store. When he saw Phyllis, he stood in front of her, clearly not ready to extend the invitation.

'Hello,' said Phyllis.

'Good afternoon,' said the doorman in a clipped voice.

She went to go around him, but he stepped sideways, blocking her path.

'I have business within,' Phyllis said, trying to sound grown-up.

'I'm very sorry, young lady. I have strict orders to allow only customers inside.' He smiled at her. 'Are you intending to buy anything today from Duckworth's?'

Phyllis frowned. 'No, but I have a friend in there and I have to see him.'

'Oh, yes?'

'Chief Inspector Inglis,' said Phyllis.

The doorman's smile started to fade. 'Chief Inspector Inglis,' he repeated.

'The guy in the window.'

The clipped tones were suddenly gone. 'And he's a friend of yours, is he?'

'I've known him for years,' Phyllis said. 'I'm helping him on the case.'

Now the doorman started looking nervous. 'You . . . you know about the . . . the *case*?' he asked.

Phyllis said nothing; she just gave him an inscrutable gaze.

'Well,' said the doorman, 'I dunno about this. I mean, I've been told . . . and if I were to—'

'Miss Wong!'

The doorman turned to see Chief Inspector Inglis emerging through the doors. 'This young lady,' he said, trying to regain his 'proper' voice, 'says she knows you, Chief Inspector.'

'That she does,' said Barry.

'I needed to see the scene of the heist. Close-up,' Phyllis said to the Inspector.

Barry and the doorman both looked around the street, and were relieved to see that there were no passers-by in the near vicinity who might have overheard Phyllis's urgent announcement.

'And,' Phyllis continued, 'I'm not going anywhere until I can.' She crossed her arms and fixed Barry Inglis with a steady look and a big smile.

It was the same smile she'd used at the top of the stairs when she'd almost killed him by groceries all those years ago. 'Well,' he said, his face starting to dissolve into the ice-down-the-pants expression Phyllis had seen a few moments earlier, 'it's highly irregular to let a civilian in to the scene of a crime, but . . . well . . . oh, good lord, Miss Wong, I guess I couldn't stop a potential customer from being *near* the scene, could I?'

'I guess you couldn't,' said Phyllis.

'Come on, then.'

The doorman sighed and stepped aside, opening one of the doors as Barry ushered Phyllis into the store.

'So, who's the dragon-lady?'

Phyllis thought she saw the Inspector almost raise a smile. 'Superintendent Marlene Parry. She's a security expert, as she keeps telling me.' He said the last bit almost under his breath, but Phyllis heard it nonetheless.

Barry took Phyllis past several counters filled with dazzling silver and gold jewellery, and staffed by elegant young women who had not a hair out of place and perfectly applied makeup on their porcelain-like faces.

'Okay, Miss Wong, if you just hover here and pretend you're looking at the things at this counter, you should be close enough to hear what's going down in the display window. It's just on the other side of this curtain.' He gestured behind him with his thumb. 'The draped doorway into the window area is there. I'll leave it open so that if by chance you find yourself eavesdropping, you won't end up straining your ears.'

'Okeydokey,' said Phyllis.

He gave her a wink and went back through the blue curtained doorway.

Phyllis kept her head tilted in the direction of the doorway, in the same way that Daisy would have inclined her small head and ears if she had been here.

The Chief Inspector was right; it was a good place to eavesdrop. And fortunately the salespeople were too busy with other customers to pay Phyllis much attention.

'It's preposterous, Chief Inspector.' Marlene Parry's voice reminded Phyllis of the least favourite teacher she'd once had. 'Not to have had any sensor detectors in this space, with a priceless necklace like that on display!'

'As I said, Superintendent, I suppose they didn't think they were necessary. Not with the armed guards who were stationed outside all through the night.'

Armed guards. Phyllis's eyes narrowed as she inspected a platinum bracelet in a display case on the counter. Barry hadn't mentioned armed guards to her when he'd shown her the footage yesterday morning.

'Armed guards are all very well,' Superintendent Parry went on, 'but they were stationed outside. Sensor detectors *in here* could've picked up on movement *within* the window.'

'Agreed,' came the Inspector's voice (a little wearily, to Phyllis's ears). 'But in the scheme of things, what good would they have done? I mean, Superintendent, you've seen the footage. You've watched it more than once—'

'Of course I have!'

'—and so you've seen that there was nobody present here. Not a soul. You saw how the Van Rockechild necklace just vanished.' Phyllis heard him click his fingers. 'Just like that!'

'*Things don't just vanish*,' said Marlene Parry in a voice that, in days long past when different forces were at work in the world, might have turned a living creature into a marble statue. 'There has to be a logical explanation. Heavens above, man, a necklace can't just be here one moment and gone the next with no sign of how it disappeared!'

'Ah,' said the Chief Inspector. 'So you *do* think it disappeared?'

'Oh, don't be ridiculous! I was using a figure of speech. It was here and then it was gone. Until we find out how that happened, and where the necklace has got to, then, to all intents and purposes, yes, it *has* disappeared. But not by any means . . . *supernatural*, Chief Inspector.'

'How can you be so sure? You saw the film; you saw how—'

'Oh, don't tell me you believe in all that mumbo-jumbo? I was told before I flew down here this morning that some officers in your force thought that there might be ghosts involved here. *Ghosts*!'

Phyllis heard her laughing—a cruel, cold laugh.

'Chief Inspector Inglis, tell me this: do you believe in ghosts?'

Phyllis listened carefully to the long pause that followed. Then she heard the Inspector's voice, strong and clear. 'Superintendent Parry, I believe in facts. I always have and I always will. And the fact of the matter here is that a piece of valuable jewellery has gone missing, and we don't for the life of us know how that happened.'

'You didn't answer my question, Chief Inspector. Do you believe in ghosts?'

'In certain cultures, ghosts are a part of life. I know *that* for a fact. And I respect that fact, Superintendent. And I think, if I may be so bold, that having respect for other people's beliefs and traditions is an important thing.'

'Ha!'

Phyllis was shocked at the machine-gun-like force of Superintendent Parry's exclamation.

'Let me ask you,' said Barry. 'What do you think happened to the Van Rockechild necklace?'

Phyllis waited for the answer, pretending to inspect a display of emerald and ruby brooches. There was a long pause. Then there was the sound of a bag being unzipped, and things being put hurriedly into it before being zipped up again.

'I've seen all I need to see here, Chief Inspector. I'll be making my report when I arrive back at my headquarters. You'll have it by tomorrow afternoon. Now, if you'll excuse me, I have a plane to catch.'

Suddenly, and without any further farewell, the dark blue drapes were swept aside and out strode Superintendent Marlene Parry. She almost knocked Phyllis over as she rushed past her.

'I bet people do cartwheels whenever they hear her name.' The Inspector stood next to Phyllis, watching the back of the Superintendent fade into the crowd of passers-by outside.

'Nah. They do handsprings, landing upon their toes.'

'Ha,' the Inspector said, without humour. 'Well, Miss Wong, that was a complete waste of a few hours of my life that I shall never get back. I hope you got something out of your little surveillance session.'

'Chief Inspector, I still need to go in there. I just want to be where it happened . . . to get a sense of the scene . . .'

‘Look, I really have to get back to the station and write up all that happened here this afternoon. I’m sorry, but—’

‘Please? I’ll only be a minute or two. I promise.’

Now Barry pulled the sort of face he would have pulled if he had just eaten a really sour lemon all in one go. He looked at his watch and sighed. ‘Okay. Two minutes, that’s it. And don’t touch anything.’ He held the velvet curtain aside.

She gave him a smile and ducked inside.

The first thing that struck Phyllis about the window area was that walking into it was how she imagined it would be to enter outer space. Everything was the same deep, dark blue colour. She took off her backpack and walked around the small space. She was surprised at how springy the carpet was. The deep blue velvet was so uniform that she almost banged into the display stand; if she hadn’t seen the fingerprint-powdered glass cube atop it, she would certainly have knocked the stand over.

Even though Barry had told her not to touch anything, she couldn’t resist: she quickly ran her hands across the drapes covering the walls. With a small, satisfied nod, she realised she’d been correct: velvet. Thick, dense velvet.

She stood in the space, then she crouched down and stood again, peering into all the corners as she walked the perimeter of the small area, carefully inspecting every place where a necklace might have been secreted. But, as the moments ticked quickly away, she felt more and more confused.

Finally, Chief Inspector Inglis parted the curtain of the doorway. 'Time's up, Miss Wong. Let's go.'

Phyllis picked up her backpack and came out. For once, she was quiet.

'Seen everything?' Barry asked.

'No,' she answered. 'I haven't. I haven't seen anything at all.'

A slight case of haberdashery

The fire was lit in the Wallace Wong cinema and the flames were casting flickers of warm yellow up onto the richly decorated walls, and onto Phyllis and Daisy as they sat in one of the plump armchairs.

Phyllis rested her head against the back of the chair and stared up at the domed ceiling. The electric stars winked and glittered. Daisy busily licked her front paws—she had just eaten her dinner and this ritual always followed when her little belly was full and she was content.

It was Saturday night and Phyllis and her dad had decided to screen *A Slight Case Of Haberdashery**, one of Wallace Wong's lesser-known pictures.

---

* *A Slight Case Of Haberdashery* (Supreme Pictures, 1932). Wallace Wong's (Conjuror of Wonder!) debut appearance in the role of hapless travelling haberdasher and amateur magician, Neddy Noblock. While the plot verges on the

(continued)

Phyllis's dad was rummaging around in the projection room, moving cans of film as he tried to locate the picture. 'It's here somewhere,' he was muttering. 'It has to be. Phyll, when was the last time we watched it?'

Phyllis thought. 'Must've been the year before last. I think I've only ever seen that one once.'

'Yes . . . not a great picture, but old Wallace shines through. Ah! Gotcha!' He took out a couple of film cans from the bottom shelf of the film cupboard, and blew the dust off them.

'Dad?'

'What, pet?' He opened up the first can and took out the reel of film.

'Do you think ghosts exist?'

'Hmmm.' He placed the reel onto the forward arm of the projector and began threading the film carefully through. 'Why do you ask?'

Phyllis knew she couldn't tell her father about the Van Rockechild heist; she'd given Chief

---

(continued)
fantastical at times (particularly in the scene where a pride of lions runs amok in the dining car of a train), the scenes with Wallace Wong still hold up well today. Believed lost for many decades, an almost complete copy of this film was discovered at the end of the 20th century in an archive on the outskirts of Paris. *(Information supplied by P.B. Botter, film historian.)*

Inspector Inglis her word that she'd keep it secret. 'Just wondering.'

'Well, I don't myself. But your grandmother and her mother did. You know that. Your grandmother used to always leave offerings and burn paper money to appease the spirits during the Chinese Ghost Festival. A lot of people still do, every July.'

'We don't.'

'No. Some rituals are better suited to others. But the belief goes back a long way. I think Confucius himself said that you should respect ghosts and gods, but keep away from them. Sounds like good advice to me, Phyll.'

Phyllis smiled and stroked Daisy behind her ear (Daisy looked up momentarily, gave Phyllis's hand a quick lick, then went back to grooming her paws). Then Phyllis frowned. 'Dad?'

'Mmmm?' He had finished threading the film onto the back spool and was about to use the blower-brush to puff away any dust from the big round lens at the front of the projector.

'Do you think things can disappear? I mean, *really* disappear . . . not as in magic, like I perform, but really, actually *vanish into the ether*?'

Harvey Wong stopped cleaning the lens and came out of the projection room. He sat in the chair beside her. 'Now, that's a good question in this family, Phyll. We never *did* find out what happened to your great-grandfather all those years ago in Venezuela. The official police report always listed him as missing. Still does, I suspect, but no evidence was ever found about how he *went* missing. And the trunk he disappeared into was just a basic gimmicked trunk like magicians use.'

'Yes?' said Phyllis, waiting for him to actually answer her question.

'Well, I suppose because of what happened in Venezuela, well . . . I guess I do believe that things . . . and people . . . can vanish. But I don't know if that's what you're asking me, is it?'

Phyllis didn't say anything, but looked up again at the twinkling electrical stars in their domed heaven.

Her father watched her, and he saw that she was trying to figure something out. 'Phyll? What's bugging you?'

She fixed him with her steady, thoughtful gaze. 'Oh, nothing. I'm just finding out that there're a lot of mysteries in this world. Things I had no idea about. Things I want to know about.'

Harvey Wong laughed.

'What's so funny?'

'Not funny,' he said. 'You just reminded me of something.'

'What?'

Her father crossed his legs and looked up at the stars. 'My dad told me the same thing about my grandfather. That Wallace wanted to know everything he could about all the mysteries out there. Oh, he had all of his magic, of course . . . and with all of that, I guess he was *creating* mysteries. But my dad told me that Wallace could never be still. He had to know what made things work. What propelled things onwards.'

'What sort of things?' asked Phyllis, intrigued.

'Bigger things. Things that he couldn't explain. The *real* mysteries. The shadowy places.'

Phyllis listened, her breathing becoming slower.

'Wallace was very much into science as well as magic, Phyll. He used to subscribe to all the science journals of his day, and go to lectures by prominent physicists and biologists and the like. And, when he was only a little older than you are now, Einstein's Theory of Relativity was accepted, and Wallace became fascinated by the whole concept of time.

'My dad told me that Wallace got hooked on the idea of the Fourth Dimension, and how our way of thinking is affected by what we call time, and how we are so influenced by time. Apparently your great-grandfather used to conduct experiments, trying to see how different ways of doing a simple thing—like dropping a heavy ball to the ground from a great height—could be affected by forces dependent on time.'

Phyllis chewed her lip. 'Huh?' she muttered.

Harvey smiled. 'I could never get my head around it all when my dad told me about it. I don't know whether *he* could either. I think he thought his father was clever, all right, but a bit hard to fathom. A bit of a mystery, like all the mysteries he was intrigued by.'

Harvey looked at his daughter. 'You know,' he said, 'it's thought that family traits often skip a generation. I think in this case, they've skipped a couple of generations. It's almost like there's a direct line from Wallace Wong, Conjuror of Wonder! to Phyllis Wong, Wonderer of the World!'

Phyllis rubbed Daisy's silky ears and grinned. She looked back up at the stars, and the flames from the fire lit up her dark eyes.

Harvey sat there with her for a few minutes, lost in thought. He didn't know whether he could answer all of her questions right now. But perhaps it was time to open up some of the other secrets that he had for her, a little earlier than he had planned.

A thread to go on

That night, after watching *A Slight Case Of Haberdashery*, Phyllis didn't sleep very well at all.

She tossed and turned, and Daisy, lying next to her on top of the blankets, found herself more than once having to shift position, each time snuggling back into her agitated friend.

When Phyllis did manage to drift off into a light and restless slumber, she dreamt of ghostly fingers reaching through a veil of star-laced gauze and snatching, *slowly* snatching, the Van Rockechild diamond necklace away into the vapor. She also dreamt of the dragon-lady, with her mean little glasses and her machine-gun laughter, standing above her and glaring down, cruelly saying with tiny flames coming out of her pinched little mouth that ghosts cannot be, they just CANNOT BE and that Chief Inspector Inglis was a fool of the highest order. And she saw Wallace Wong, floating around a galaxy filled with loudly ticking clocks and oversized pocket-watches. Or sometimes, for some strange reason, Phyllis dreamt of jelly.

Then, just before the dawn broke, she dreamt of the Duckworth window display. She found herself gliding through all of the dense-as-midnight blue velvet, and then suddenly she was falling into the never-ending colour, down, down, down, as though she had plummeted into a black hole in some vast velvety galaxy from which she would never return.

Phyllis woke from that dream, sitting bolt upright in her bed in a cold sweat, and with an idea.

Maybe she needed to think about things from a different angle . . .

Minette Bulbolos answered the door, blinking at the dimly silhouetted figure on the landing.

'Hi,' said Phyllis. 'I hope I didn't get you up or anything.'

Minette ran a hand through her dark, bed-tangled hair. 'Oh, good morning, my *habibi*. What is the time?'

'It's 9:30,' said Phyllis.

'Ah.' Minette arched her back and stretched,

her crimson silk dressing gown shimmering sleekly. 'Then it is time to face the daylight! Come in, Phyllis, come and have some breakfast with me, yes?'

She held the door open wide and gestured theatrically for Phyllis to enter.

Phyllis had never been inside Minette's apartment, but it was very much what she had imagined it would be like: a mixture of chic furniture that was a little on the shabby side (but still very smart to look at) and old things like glass lamps and small bronze figurines and a dress mannequin in the corner and large, brilliantly coloured fans hanging on the walls. A pair of diaphanous shawls covered the back of a generous lounge in the centre of the sitting room. Long silk wrappings, feather boas and sparkly lengths of shimmery-looking fabric were dotted around the room, some of them hanging from the curtain rods, some of them draped over table lamps, some lying like coiled snakes on the Turkish rug in the middle of the floor.

'I'll just make some toast,' said Minette. 'Fancy a slice?'

'Thanks, but I just had breakfast at the café.'

'Ah, the pastries down there are to die for!' She winked at Phyllis. 'Please, sit, make yourself at home. And—' she fluttered her heavy eyelashes— 'tell me what has brought you here.'

Phyllis sat on the lounge and promptly sank deep into the cushions, squirming a little.

Minette laughed. 'Ah! I have been meaning for *years* to get that thing re-upholstered. It is one of the reasons I do not keep a small pet like your gorgeous Daisy. I am sure it would be swallowed up whole in there!'

Minette ducked into the kitchen, where she started fixing breakfast and from where she could see Phyllis as they talked. 'So, what can I do for you this morning?'

'I need some help,' said Phyllis, tucking one leg underneath her to try to avoid a partial submergence into the lounge.

'Anything I can do, for you I shall do it.' Minette filled the kettle and began rummaging around in the refrigerator.

'I need to get some info,' Phyllis told her. 'There's something I want to find out from Duckworth's.'

Minette popped her head round the door of the kitchen, her full lips spreading into a smile. 'Duckworth's, eh? Or Sparkleville, as my friend Nina calls it. Well, Phyllis, now you're talking!'

Phyllis smiled back. She would have asked the Chief Inspector to help her with this, but he had been called away, out of town, on investigative business.

'What sort of info?' asked Minette.

'I liked the colour of the velvet they used in a window display I saw, and I want to find out who put up the display for them.'

'Uh-huh.' Minette started making her toast.

'And they're a bit . . . funny . . . when it comes to kids my age. It's almost impossible to get in there if you're not an adult. They've got doormen with attitude.'

'Oh, yes. They certainly do.'

'And if they won't let me into the store, they probably won't talk to me on the phone either. So I was wondering, would you be able to call them and ask who did the window display? It was the one they had for the Van Rockechild necklace last week . . .'

Minette appeared in the doorway. 'Oh, Phyllis, I'll do better than that. I'll go in there in person and speak to the manager.'

'Really? I don't want to put you to any trouble, Minette.'

'Trouble? Since when is getting the chance to look at the most beautiful jewellery this side of Tutankhamun's tomb *trouble*? Oh, any excuse to visit Duckworth's, my sweet. I'll go this morning, as soon as they open! And you will come with me. Yes, you will come into the store with me and we will speak to the manager and find out the information you seek and look at the jewellery and the gems and have a fine time of it! And, my *habibi*, don't you worry about those doormen with the attitude. Attitude can be met head-on! And, believe me, I know how to do *just* that.'

Phyllis and Minette approached the gleaming front doors of Duckworth's shortly after the store opened.

Minette was wearing a black dress, black high-heeled shoes and big dark sunglasses. If Clement could have seen her, his reaction probably would have alerted seismologists. As Minette walked along the sidewalk, many people could not help but stare at her, no doubt wondering what movie they had seen her in.

They stopped outside the store. 'Ah, here we are, Phyllis. Sparkleville itself!' Minette looked at Phyllis over the top of her sunglasses and raised her dark, finely pencilled eyebrows.

For some reason Phyllis felt uneasy as she stood looking at the store. She hadn't been made to feel welcome last time and now, without the Chief Inspector there in his official capacity, she felt the desire to go in begin to ebb away like a receding tide.

'Minette, do you mind if I don't go in with you?'

Minette pulled her sunglasses down her nose and regarded her young friend. 'You don't want to?'

Phyllis shrugged. 'I . . . I feel . . . out of place in there,' she said. 'I mean, I guess jewellery and all that glamorous stuff isn't me. Not yet, anyway.'

Minette put her arm around Phyllis's shoulders. 'I understand, my dear *habibi.* Don't you worry about it one little ouncette! You wait outside and I'll go in and find the manager and get the goss. Then I'll come straight out and tell you what I've discovered. After that we'll go and do something you want to do. How about that?'

'You're swell, you are,' Phyllis said.

'Ah!' Minette laughed. 'You have such funny words sometimes. Look, there is a park bench there. You make yourself comfortable and I'll duck into Sparkleville.' She winked and pushed her sunglasses back up her nose.

'Sounds good.'

'I promise I won't be too long.' With that, she lifted her chin and walked towards the doorman.

Phyllis sat on the bench and watched Minette, with her shoulders pushed back and her head held high, sail like a beautiful galleon up to the doorman.

He took a small step back from her as she came closer, then Phyllis saw a huge smile erupt across his face. He held the door open and, with a wave of his gloved hand, gestured for Minette to enter.

Phyllis shook her head and grinned. Now she knew what Minette meant about meeting attitude head-on.

For the next few minutes Phyllis watched the Sunday morning shoppers come and go, and she observed the way the late morning light fell across the buildings opposite. She loved seeing how, at different times of the day, various buildings took on different appearances as the light shifted and moved across them. She sometimes thought that if she weren't so focussed on her magic, she'd take up painting and do a whole series of watercolours of her favourite city buildings in their different moods.

The wind began to pick up, sweeping a clump of dead leaves along the gutter like a dry, crackling stream. Phyllis pulled her coat more tightly around her, and was glad to see the doorman open the door and tip his hat to the emerging Minette.

'Mission accomplished,' she said as she sat next to Phyllis.

'What's the story?'

'Well, I got to see the manager and he was very

helpful. He said that Duckworth's didn't create the display for the Van Rockechild necklace. They always get a specialist display company for their really important displays.'

'So what's the company?'

'It was contracted out to the Superb Brothers.'

Phyllis looked at her. 'The Superb Brothers?'

'Yes.' Minette took some lipstick from her shoulder bag and began putting it on. 'I've heard of them, my petal. They supply a lot of very zhooshy fabrics and glittery materials for the cabarets around town. My friend Nina gets all her plumes from them.'

'Where are they?'

Minette finished applying her lipstick. She smacked her lips gently, put the lipstick back into her bag and took out a small business card. 'Here,' she said, giving it to Phyllis. 'The manager gave it to me. They're not far uptown.'

Phyllis looked at the card. '"Superb Bros. Fabrics and Textiles of Exotica",' she read aloud. '"*Suppliers to stage, screen and a discerning clientele. Sequins, feathers and spangles our speciality. Open 7 days.*"'

'Yes,' said Minette. 'My friend Nina is one of their "discerning clientele". She is very fussy about her feathers. Once she had a headdress filled with plumes from the bird of paradise; the brightest array of colours you ever did see. But she didn't get it from the Superb Brothers and she had the nastiest rash for weeks, like a map of Uruguay all up and down her neck and cheeks,' she confided gravely. 'Show business can have its dangers, Phyllis, dangers that no one can predict—'

'Minette?'

'Mmm?'

'You know how you said we could do something I'd like?'

Minette turned to her. 'Oh, yes. What do you feel like? Some cakes? A movie? A little retail therapy perhaps?'

'Let's go and see the Superb Brothers.'

Display's the thing

When Phyllis and Minette walked into Superb Brothers Fabrics and Textiles of Exotica and saw the two men behind the counter, Phyllis was glad that she was with her friend.

The two men were almost identical. They were both thin and blue-eyed and were, Phyllis imagined, aged somewhere in their seventies. Both of them had jet-black hair which, the young magician thought, could not have been a natural state of play at their age. The jet-black also extended to their neatly trimmed pencil-thin moustaches.

Both men wore name tags on their blazers; *Marvin* on one and *Mervyn* on the other. Marvin was standing, organising some diamante-type buttons sewn onto cardboard backings, and Mervyn was sitting, adding up the quantities that Marvin was counting.

As soon as they saw Phyllis they stopped what they were doing and their lips pursed so tightly that she thought she could have put her spare change in there.

'Yes?' said Marvin, looking down his nose at her. Clearly a person of Phyllis's age was not welcome in this establishment any more than at Duckworth's.

'Good afternoon,' Minette said, her voice oozing warmth. 'How do you do?'

Marvin and Mervyn looked up at Minette and their lips lost their pursedness. Suddenly the men's faces were awash with beaming, professional smiles.

'Good afternoon, madam,' Marvin greeted Minette. 'How may we be of assistance?'

Phyllis observed the way both men looked Minette up and down appreciatively.

'Ah,' said Minette. 'I have heard of your wonderful store from one of my colleagues. She buys all of her feathers and sparklies from you. I have been meaning to pay you a visit for a long time . . . and now, here I am, with my young friend.' Minette looked past the counter to the rest of the shop. 'What treasures you have!'

The shop was lined with wooden shelves from ceiling to floor, and every shelf was filled with bolts of silk and velvet and sateen and tulle and sparkling organza. Long banners dotted with sequins in every colour imaginable hung here and there between the shelving. A dozen mannequins stood frozen about the place, their limbs draped with diaphanous golden or silver or green cloths, or bright crimson or yellow boas, and their heads festooned with brilliantly coloured feathers.

Phyllis imagined that when Wallace Wong was performing, his assistants might have come to a place such as Superb Bros. to get fitted out. That thought warmed her; it was as if she had come across a connection with her past.

'More treasures than Aladdin's cave,' Marvin said.

Mervyn said nothing, but arched an eyebrow and nodded his head slowly.

'Is there anything,' Marvin asked, 'in *particular* you are looking for?'

Minette sighed. 'Oh, if only I had come in here three weeks ago. I have just had new outfits made for my act, but if I had taken my friend Nina's advice I would have bought my material from you. Next time, for sure.'

'We have the finest selection for the theatre and cabaret, and we also cater to those in the *burlesque realms*,' said Marvin, his smile fading ever so slightly as he began to realise that perhaps Minette wasn't going to be making any purchases today.

Mervyn nodded.

'I will certainly return,' said Minette.

Phyllis gave Minette's arm a small nudge.

'Oh,' Minette said, as if she'd just had a thought. 'There *is* something you may be able to help me with. I recently saw the most wonderful display in the window of Duckworth's. The Van Rockechild diamond necklace display, and I couldn't help admiring how simply *sumptuous* the draperies were . . .'

Marvin smiled a watery smile. 'Ah, yes?'

Mervyn nodded, the inside corners of his eyebrows rising.

'. . . the most deep blue, very rich and dark. You wouldn't know where I could find that sort of drape, would you?'

'Well,' said Marvin, clasping his hands and rubbing them gently together, 'you have come to the right place, madam. We here at Superb Bros. were the designers and fitters for that very display.'

Mervyn nodded proudly and raised the outer corners of his eyebrows.

'Oh, did you hear that, Phyllis?' Minette said. 'Fancy!'

'Fancy indeed,' Phyllis said, trying not to grin.

'Oh, yes,' Marvin went on. 'Duckworth's is one

of our . . . *better* . . . clients. They always call on us when they want to do a major window dressing. We have been servicing them for . . . ooh, how long, Mervyn? At least twenty years?'

Mervyn thought for a second, then nodded in confirmation.

'Yes,' said Marvin. 'It was one of our best displays of late, if I do say so myself. I chose the colour of the background especially to showcase the brrrrrilliance of the necklace.' He rolled his *rrrrr*s so suddenly that Phyllis's shoulders shot up.

'Oh, yes,' said Minette. 'We both thought the necklace was displayed to its most dazzling advantage. Didn't we, Phyllis?'

'Mm-hm,' said Phyllis. 'Dazzling.'

Mervyn nodded at Phyllis, as if to say, 'Well of course it was; we are experts, after all.'

Marvin said, 'Would you care for some of that velvet, madam? I do believe we have a small quantity still available.'

'Well, if you have some . . .' Minette smiled and gave Phyllis a small wink.

Marvin clicked his fingers at Mervyn, who nodded and drifted off to the rear of the store.

'Yes, it is the most plush velvet on the market,' Marvin told them while they waited for Mervyn. 'Triple velvet. We import it from Istanbul. Very hard to get, on account of its rarity and the time it takes to weave.'

'Ah,' said Minette. 'It is indeed precious.'

Mervyn appeared at the counter again, holding a long bolt of the deep blue velvet. He placed it onto the counter and unrolled it with the smooth, seamless action of a man who has been doing such a thing for at least fifty years.

'There,' said Marvin. 'Indulge your fingertips, madam. Feel the luxuriousness of that!'

Minette reached out and ran her fingers across the velvet. Phyllis also reached out, but Mervyn gave her such a glare that his eyebrows bristled and seemed ready to leap out at her. She quickly reconsidered.

'Yes, it is very luxurious,' Minette said.

Mervyn nodded at her to acknowledge her good taste.

'Would madam like a small length?' asked Marvin with a gleam in his eye.

'Madam would,' Minette answered. 'Have you a metre there?'

'One metre,' repeated Marvin. He pointed to Mervyn, who withdrew a pair of long-bladed scissors from below the counter. He held the velvet against the ruler inlaid into the countertop and proceeded to snip off the required length.

'Tell me,' said Minette, 'did you hang all the draperies in the Duckworth's window yourselves?'

'Ah, no, madam.' Marvin watched Mervyn snipping. 'Long gone are the days of us doing the window fittings ourselves. No, we have contractors who do it for us nowadays. To our *exact* instructions, of course. Our reputation is second-to-none.'

Mervyn had finished cutting the length and was folding the fabric neatly.

'Actually,' Marvin confided, 'it was a miracle the Duckworth's display looked as fine as it did. We had to use a new lot of fitters for that job—our regular boys were on vacation in Acapulco. So we found another team through an employment agency. Ugh! Never again! Oh, they did the job all right, but—oh! The appearance of them! We were shocked when we went to supervise. One of them looked like he'd been through the dishwasher, didn't he?'

Mervyn nodded, wincing slightly as he wrapped the velvet in brown paper.

'Oooh, yes,' Marvin said, screwing up his nose so that his thin moustache splayed outwards. 'He had this *ghastly* scar . . . sort of pale brown, verging on red . . . ran all the way from here to here . . .'

Phyllis watched as he drew a line with his finger from the corner of his right eye to nearly halfway down his cheek.

And her blood ran as cold as ice!

'We *do* have a reputation to maintain,' Marvin said. 'We don't want scruffbuckets or rough-looking types representing Superb Bros. We complained to the employment agency, but they had no idea what we were talking about. They said they didn't have such a person on their books. Hmph. We'll never use *that* agency again when we need men to fit for us!'

'Phyllis! Are you all right?'

Phyllis's legs had gone hollow, and she had to grip the edge of the counter to stop herself from swooning.

'Yes,' she said quietly. 'I just need some fresh air.'

'Oh, you're not going to throw up, are you?' asked Marvin, alarmed.

'No,' Minette said. 'I will take her outside. How much do I owe you gentlemen?'

'Sixty-five dollars, thank you,' said Marvin, abruptly.

Minette handed over the exact amount. 'Thank you,' she said, taking her parcel and leading Phyllis out of the shop.

'Oh, thank *you*,' said Marvin as she went through the door. 'And do come again. *You*, madam, are more than welcome.'

To which Mervyn nodded and raised his eyebrows in a manner that clearly dismissed Minette and Phyllis.

Outside, the wind had picked up and a bitter chill was lacing every gust. 'Hmm,' said Minette. 'Marvin and Mervyn. A pair of right mavens, it seems to me.'

Phyllis was silent as she stared at the sidewalk.

'My *habibi*? Are you all right? You are as pale as snow! Come, come, I will take you to a café and get you some water and something to eat. Something chocolatey perhaps. Then I will take you safely home.'

But the dread that was spreading through Phyllis refused to be comforted. She felt decidedly ill.

If only there were xylophones . . .

Phyllis Wong did not sleep that night. Her mind had been catapulted back to frock-coat guy and what he was up to.

She reasoned at first that perhaps it wasn't him. Maybe the man with the scar whom the Superb Brothers had told her and Minette about was another man with a scar similar to frock-coat guy's. But the more Phyllis thought about it, the more she felt deep down that it *had* to be frock-coat guy. A scar like that isn't common, and the strangeness of the thefts—the substitution of Mrs Lowerblast's blue wren bookend and the disappearance of the Van Rockechild necklace—were too similar, too . . . *weird* . . . for it not to be the same man.

Phyllis again began to fear that he would return to Mrs Lowerblast's store to nab the other bookend. Even though there was a back-to-base alarm system now, Phyllis couldn't help feeling that there was danger ahead. She could sense it in the very marrow of her bones.

Daisy had stayed awake for much of the night, too. She picked up on Phyllis's fear and uneasiness, and if Phyllis couldn't sleep, then neither could she. The humans had to be settled before she could be; that was one of her core responsibilities in the Wong household, and she took her responsibilities very seriously, as any loyal dog always does.

School the next day was all but a write-off. Phyllis couldn't concentrate on anything her teachers were saying, and by lunchtime she was feeling strange and disoriented.

Some of her close friends realised that Phyllis wasn't her normal, outgoing self. They tried to coax her into performing a trick or two, but Phyllis gave them a half-hearted smile and told them she didn't have any props with her (which wasn't true—she always had at least one deck of cards, some sponge balls, silk handkerchiefs and special coins in a secret compartment in her backpack).

It was only when she was walking home with Clement that she started to open up a bit. He knew about frock-coat guy, but not about the necklace heist. She needed to let him know what she was thinking, if only to share the burden of what she was suspecting.

'Are you sure it's the same man?' he asked as they made their way down one of the wide avenues that led to their neighbourhood.

'Has to be.' Phyllis meandered along, frowning and kicking at the leaves. 'The second crime is too similar to Mrs L.'s. They're both too peculiar.'

'So what was taken from the second place?' Suddenly he stopped walking and his mouth fell open. 'Hey! I bet whatever it was it got stolen from Duckworth's! That's why you went there the other day. That must be why. The Phyllis Wong I know isn't into jewellery and all that girl stuff!'

She stopped walking and took a deep breath. 'Okay, Clem, I'll level with you. But you've got to promise me one thing.'

He drew a cross over his shirt with an ink-stained finger. 'Cross my aorta nineteen different ways,' he said. 'What?'

'That you won't breathe a word of this to anybody. Not even your mum. I gave Chief Inspector Inglis a promise, you understand.'

'Mum's the word,' he said. 'Or, in this case, *not*.'

'C'mon.' She started off up the sidewalk again, and he hurried alongside her. 'You're right,' she said. 'The second crime did take place at Duckworth's.'

'What was nabbed?'

Phyllis told him, and she told him how it had disappeared, and that she had seen the actual disappearance over and over on the CCTV footage. When she mentioned that some of the police force thought ghosts might've been involved, Clement whistled loudly.

'Ooh, man! Ghosts?' he said worriedly. 'What do you think?'

'No,' Phyllis answered. 'It's not ghosts. It's some other explanation.'

'Like what?'

'I have absolutely no idea. None at all. But from my enquiries, I'm almost certain that it was pulled off by the same guy who robbed Mrs Lowerblast.'

'C'mon,' said Clement. 'Let's take the alleyway. I'm cold. I left my sweater somewhere at school. Again.'

Phyllis said nothing, but followed him into the long, narrow alleyway which they sometimes used as a shortcut home.

'So what can you do now?' he asked her as they walked past a row of trash cans and a big pile of empty cardboard boxes that were waiting to be rained on.

'I have to talk to the Inspector again. I've got to tell him what I've found out from the Superb Brothers. Maybe he can investigate further and find the employment agency that the Superbs used for the Duckworth's display. Maybe that's got something to do with it. It's the only thing I can think of.'

They were almost at the end of the alleyway now, just before it turned the corner into the side street where they were headed. The high walls all around them had cut off the sun's rays, and the whole place had a dingy, shadowy feel to it.

Then Clement stopped. 'What the—?'

Phyllis stopped too, as she saw what was approaching from around the corner.

As far as the City's street sweeping machines went, this was one of the biggest, one of the tallest, one of the chunkiest, one of the most powerful. It was barrelling down towards them, tearing through the alleyway at a monstrous speed, its two enormous rotating brushes at the front and the four along the sides blasting at full power as the vehicle squeezed between the walls of the alley.

'It's not gonna stop!' yelled Clement above the engine and the deafening swish of the brushes.

Phyllis froze as she saw, through the grimy window of the driver's cabin, a man with a smile that seemed to spew malevolence at her and Clement.

The street sweeper hurtled closer, the noise from its diesel engine fouling the air as the SWOOSH SWOOSH SWOOOOOOOSH of its brushes ripped through the alley.

Phyllis shook her head. 'Let's take it on the lam!' she cried.

'What?' shouted Clement.

'RUN!'

She grabbed him, spun him round and pulled him along. Together they started racing away from the monster that was bearing down upon them.

Clement dropped his backpack and he heard, above the machine's din, the sickening crack of his laptop. 'Oh, *noooo*—'

'Clem! *Run*! You can't stop!'

They kept racing, trying to out-run the machine, but the sweeper gave a sudden mighty roar as the engine was opened up to full power. On it came at them, bearing down faster and faster, and they could feel the blast of the hot air from the frenzied brushes against their backs.

That's when Phyllis lost her footing.

And fell.

Clement saw this and dived down onto the ground next to her just as one of the mighty brushes swept up against him and Phyllis, and as the sweeper was about to drive right over them, he pushed and rolled Phyllis away, out towards the side of the alleyway.

They crashed hard into the tower of cardboard boxes and the whole lot came tumbling down on top of them.

For what seemed like hours, there was no movement. Phyllis stayed under the boxes with Clement, listening as the noise of the street sweeper seemed to fade away into the distance.

Then, when she thought it was safe, Phyllis pushed the boxes off them and crawled out.

The street sweeper was nowhere to be seen.

'Clem! You were brilliant! You saved us.' She kept her eye on the alley, and spoke in a whisper. 'Did you see the driver? He had the scar, Clem . . . and the monocle . . . C'mon, let's get out of here!'

But when she turned back, offering her hand to help him up, she felt her stomach lurch.

Clement was just lying there, twisted and small. One of his legs was at an impossible angle to the rest of his body.

'Clem! Are you okay?'

He opened one eye, slowly.

'Are you all right?'

'My leg . . . I can't . . .'

'Clem! Clem!'

And then everything went black.

PART THREE

A bigger sort of magic

What went down

'It was an Algin Whirlwind street sweeper, Mr Wong. Reported stolen from the City Council depot last week. One of the patrol squads found it abandoned by the wharves late yesterday afternoon. A lot of damage to the side of the vehicle, apparently.'

'I see,' said Phyllis's father, sounding tired and stressed. 'Thank you for coming to tell me of this, Chief Inspector.'

Barry Inglis sat uncomfortably opposite him. It was Wednesday afternoon and he had called in on his way to work. Even though the theft of a street sweeper did not come under the mandate of the Fine Arts and Antiques Squad of the Metropolitan Police, he had taken a personal interest in the case and had insisted on keeping Mr Wong in the loop.

'They've fingerprinted the vehicle,' he continued, running his thumbs down the freshly laundered creases in his trousers, 'and forensics have gone over it inch by inch, but nothing has turned up. We're trying to find out who the low-life perpetrator is, but all we've got to go on is what Miss Wong . . . er, Phyllis, told us before she—'

He stopped, and Harvey Wong watched as the detective's face almost—*almost*—crumpled. But in a second, Barry Inglis had taken a big, steadying breath, and his voice had resumed its hard, slightly weary tone. 'Before this awful business went down.'

'I see,' said Harvey Wong. 'More tea, Chief Inspector?'

'No, thank you. I really should be getting to the station.'

Harvey Wong stood. 'Of course. Again, thank you for coming to visit me.'

'All part of the job, sir,' said Barry, standing also. He started for the door, then stopped. 'I'm so very sorry about all of this,' he said. 'I just want you to know that. And I want you to know that we'll find the perpetrator, and he'll rue the day he was born.'

Harvey Wong nodded. 'It certainly does not seem like it was any sort of accident.'

'No,' Barry answered. 'I don't believe it was. But keep that under your hat. I think there was intent. And that's why we're making this top priority. If there's a madman loose in the city, hunting down innocent young people like Miss W—Phyllis—and her friend, he's got to be apprehended as soon as . . .' His voice trailed off, and he took another deep breath. Then, in a soft voice, he asked, 'Mr Wong, how is she?'

'Ah, Chief Inspector, perhaps you would like to see for yourself?'

If Barry Inglis had not been such a seasoned police officer he would have perhaps done a little skip on the spot at that moment. 'Well, if it's at all convenient . . . yes, I would, Mr Wong.'

Harvey smiled and went to the door. 'Phyll!' he called up the hallway. 'Someone here to see you!'

'Who?' came Phyllis's voice.

'Come and find out.'

'An Inspector calls,' Barry Inglis shouted in an unexpected outburst of enthusiasm. He quickly looked a little embarrassed. 'Oh, I'm sorry, Mr Wong. I don't know where that came from. Must've been something I ate,' he said, trying to make light of it.

'That's quite all right,' said Harvey Wong, smiling.

There were footsteps in the hall, and then Phyllis appeared in the doorway. Daisy trotted along nimbly beside her, her small snout raised high.

'Hello,' Phyllis said when she saw the Chief Inspector.

'Hello to you. It's good to see you up and about. But, young Clement's broken in three places, eh? Good lord, what a business.'

Phyllis sat in one of the lounge chairs. 'I always tell him to go for the big finish,' she said quietly. 'Just like Wallace Wong used to.'

Daisy sprang up into Phyllis's lap and sat there like a miniature sphinx, her dark brown eyes fixed firmly on Chief Inspector Inglis.

'Hello, Daisy.' Barry gave her a small pat, and she almost purred appreciatively.

'Inspector Inglis was just telling me about the street sweeper,' Phyllis's dad told her.

Phyllis stroked Daisy's head slowly and gently between her ears. 'What about it?' she asked.

The Inspector told Phyllis what he had told Harvey Wong. She listened with a faraway look in her eyes.

'. . . and, as I said to your dad, we couldn't find any sign of the driver. No prints or traces of anything.'

Phyllis's eyes became steely as she stared at the rug beneath her feet.

'Miss Wong, this isn't an official visit, but may I ask you something?'

She didn't say anything, but continued staring at the rug.

Chief Inspector Inglis looked at Harvey Wong, who gave a small nod, as if to tell him to go ahead.

'Well,' said the Inspector, 'Clement told us when we interviewed him that you saw the driver. Did you get a good look? Good enough to identify him if you saw him again?'

'Didn't he tell you what I said?' Phyllis asked, her eyes still fixed on the rug.

'He did.' The Inspector went and sat on an ottoman in front of her chair. 'But I'd like to hear it from you. Just in case something got left out . . .'

'Go on, Phyll,' said her father.

Phyllis stopped stroking Daisy. She intertwined her thumb and little finger and clasped the backs of her hands tightly. 'I saw him, all right,' she said in a voice barely louder than a whisper. 'I saw him. I know who it was.'

Barry Inglis leant forward. 'You know him?'

'I know who it was.'

'Who?' Barry asked quietly.

Phyllis squeezed her hands together until her knuckles turned white. 'It was the frock-coat guy. The guy who did Mrs L. over, and who was involved with the Duckworth's job.'

The Inspector blinked. 'The Duckworth's job? How do you know he was—?'

'The scar. I'm sure he was in on it.'

Barry pulled out a notepad and pen and started writing. 'I'll get to that later. Just tell me, did you see his frock coat when he was coming at you?'

Phyllis shook her head. 'I didn't see what he was wearing.'

'Then how do you know—?'

She slowly raised her eyes and looked at him. 'I saw his scar, Chief Inspector. And he was wearing the monocle. I saw it glinting as he was about to—' She stopped and took a deep, shuddering breath.

Daisy peered up at Phyllis's face and started licking her hands, trying to soothe her.

Barry Inglis noted down the details. 'I see. That's very useful to know. Very useful indeed.'

Harvey Wong said, 'I think perhaps that Phyllis should rest now. She's still feeling some shock, I think. She has a way to go before she will be fully recovered.'

Barry stood. 'Of course.' He put his notepad and pen in his pocket. 'Thanks for talking,' he said to Phyllis. 'I've got to be getting in to headquarters. There's all sorts of business going down . . . a new Picasso painting's about to be unveiled at the

Metropolitan Art Gallery next month, and you wouldn't believe the paperwork and the planning we have to do.'

'A new Picasso?' asked Harvey Wong, surprised. 'Goodness me.'

'Well,' said the Chief Inspector, heading for the door, 'not exactly *new*. I mean, the guy's been dead for years. But this one's only recently been discovered in some deceased estate in Switzerland, and the Gallery bought it. Paid a small fortune. Actually, make that a *large* fortune. It'll be the first time it's been on public display in over seventy years. The opening will be a big occasion if you like *hors d'oeuvres*.' He pronounced it as 'horse doovers' and gave Phyllis a wink.

She made a small grunting sound and unlocked her hands to stroke Daisy once more between her ears.

'I'll talk to you again when you're feeling better,' he said. 'About the Duckworth's connection. Goodbye for now.'

'Bye,' said Phyllis quietly.

'Thank you, Chief Inspector.' Harvey Wong escorted him out into the hallway.

'You're welcome,' said Barry, shaking his hand.

As Barry walked down the stairs he couldn't help but think that the Phyllis he had just spoken to wasn't the Phyllis he knew. There was a dullness in her eyes, and her voice had sounded . . . smaller. It didn't have the confident, clear ring to it that he was used to.

Probably shock, he thought. *She's still getting over it. It's a hell of a thing to happen to anyone, let alone a couple of kids . . .*

❃

Phyllis's father kept her home from school on Thursday and Friday. She was sleeping a lot and still didn't seem her usual self.

When she wasn't sleeping Phyllis spent the time wandering from one room to the next, but she didn't feel like occupying herself with anything much. Not even the arrival in the mail of a new Oriental Die Cabinet with bright red and yellow die and a deep walnut veneer which she had ordered from a magic shop in Paris aroused much enthusiasm. She unwrapped it and put it on the shelves in her room, alongside all her other magic props and tricks.

Daisy stayed constantly by her side, or at her feet, or on her lap, or curled up next to her on her bed when she was sleeping. The little dog knew that her friend was not her usual self, and she kept a protective (and sometimes a licking and grooming) vigil over Phyllis during the days and nights.

There was nothing Phyllis wanted to do right now, but shut her eyes and pretend she wasn't anywhere at all.

❃

'Ha!' laughed Clement. 'Even I could do better than that!'

On the weekend Harvey Wong insisted that Phyllis get out into the sunshine. He was concerned that she was becoming paler and paler, and had arranged with Clement's parents for Clement and Phyllis to spend the afternoon in City Park. Now Phyllis, Clement and Daisy were sitting in a sheltered spot by the statue of the politician with his weasel. Daisy was snuggled up on the soft grass next to Clement's crutches as Phyllis leant against the trunk of a big tree.

'Better than what?' she asked, not really interested as she half-heartedly watched some joggers passing.

'This.' He poked his glasses further up his nose and swivelled his webPad around to show her what he'd been looking at. '*The Weeping Walrus* by a guy called Picasso. It's on the news page. Man, the walrus looks like it went into a bar and never came out again! They should never serve walruses alcohol, if you ask me. Bleeerrrrgh!'

Phyllis looked at the screen, and Daisy poked her snout close to it. Phyllis saw a strange, distorted figure, all green and light purple with smears of crimson here and there. One of its eyes was where its ear might have been if it had been human, and the other eye was winking down near its mouth, which was wide and slash-like across the fleshy face. The body was even weirder. Phyllis couldn't work out whether it was that of a woman or a large sea-going creature.

'He should've put clothes on it,' said Clement, smirking.

'What's it say about it?' she asked, leaning back against the tree.

Clement turned the webPad around and scrolled down. 'It just says it's going on display next month and there'll be a gala opening night, blah blah blah. Hey, why d'you think people would want to go out and see *that* when they can just look at it on their computer or their webPad or their phone? That's what I'd rather do.'

'People are strange, I guess,' said Phyllis.

Clement turned off the webPad and shoved it into his backpack. 'Hey, Phyll, you wanna draw on my plaster? I'll bet you can do a better Weeping Walrus than that Picasso guy. *I* sure could.'

'Yeah, but you're good at drawing. Always have been.'

'Go on, I've got some pens here and—'

'No thanks, Clem. Not today.'

He frowned. 'You remind me of that horse.'

'What horse?'

'That horse in that joke.'

Phyllis looked at him.

'You know,' he told her. 'A horse goes into a bar and orders a drink. The barman says, "Hey, why the long face?" and the horse says, "I'm a horse!"' Clement sniggered loudly.

Phyllis said nothing.

'Aw, c'mon, Phyll. Lighten up. *I'm* the one with the crutches, not you. Things'll get better, you know.'

'Yeah. Sure.' It was all she could do to stop a tear forming in the corner of her eye.

What they said

'Has Phyllis been in lately, Pascaline?'

Mrs Lowerblast was about to tuck into the large slice of *mille-feuille* which Pascaline had just set down in front of her.

'Ooh, *non*, *Madame*. She 'as nert been in 'ere for nearly ze fortnight now.'

'Poor girl. Such a dreadful business.'

'*Oui*. I zink she 'as taken eet very badly. I see 'er cerming 'ome frerm school sermtimes, bert she no lernger gives me a *bonjour* or even ze wave. She jerst goes into ze lobby wiz 'er 'ead dern, looking at ze floor . . .'

'Hmmm.' Mrs Lowerblast stared at the pastry. Suddenly the chocolate on top and the vanilla icing didn't seem all that appealing, even though this was one of her favourite sweets at The Délicieux Café.

'Maybe,' said Pascaline, her brow furrowed, 'she will start getting better when 'er *ami* Clement 'as ze plaster erf frerm 'is leg? Maybe zat will 'elp her lerk at zings differently, and she can move onwards . . .'

'*Ja*, maybe,' said Mrs Lowerblast. 'This we can only hope. And we can only be around, if she needs us.'

'*Oui*,' said Pierre, from the kitchen. 'Zat we merst.'

No time for Neddy

The platinum-blonde woman approaches the stage door from the dingy alley at the back of the theatre.

Neddy Noblock, the dapper but shy stage door attendant, nervously watches her through the spy window in the door. He's been watching her for months now, but hasn't managed to pluck up the courage to speak to her. After all, why would Bunny van der Doodle, the lead dancing girl in the Marlowe Follies, want to waste her time getting to know a mere doorman like Neddy Noblock?

But tonight is different. Tonight Neddy has made up his mind. He's summoned up every known ounce of courage (and some other ounces he never knew he had) and he's made the decision: he's going to ask her out!

He can hear her high heels click-click-click*ing up the alley as she comes nearer. He rubs his thin moustache, neatening it with the tips of his index* *fingers. He brushes a hand across his hair. He straightens his necktie.*

Then—oh horror!—he realises he hasn't got his coat on. He's in his shirt sleeves!

'Gracious me,' he mutters. 'My coat!'

His eyes widen as he tries to remember where he put the coat when he took it off earlier this evening.

He searches frantically as the click-click-click*ing of Bunny's towering heels comes nearer, the sound amplifying as it bounces off the walls of the narrow alley.*

Where is it?

The coat is not hanging on the hook behind his small desk and chair, the place he usually slings it when he arrives for work. He ducks and looks under the desk. Nothing. He looks on the prop baskets and trunks leading to the wings, on the hooks along the walls by the dressing rooms, in every dim nook and backstage cranny.

Neddy Noblock's plaid coat is nowhere to be seen!

In desperation—for he must look his best for this monumental moment—he dives into the first dressing room he comes to. Luckily it is empty. He sees what he needs: a dinner jacket, deep black with silk lapels, hanging on a stand. He quickly gives it the once-over and decides that it might just fit.

He whips it off the stand and slips into it as smoothly as an eel into a lake of unset jelly. Then he turns and rushes back to the stage door.

Just in time. As he buttons the dinner jacket, the buzzer at the door sounds. Neddy takes a deep, fortifying breath. Does that sound herald the beginning of the rest of his life, a life that may change with the glorious prospect of—?

The buzzer sounds again, impatiently, like a small child demanding that the world attends to its every whim, now, right this second!

Neddy Noblock is sweating. He opens the door and smiles at Bunny van der Doodle.

Her steel-grey eyes, with brilliant quartz-like flecks, flash at him. 'What took you so long?' she asks. Her voice is like a lazy river with nowhere particular to flow.

'Good evening, Miss van der Doodle,' says Neddy. 'I'm sorry. Please come in.'

He steps back and gives a small bow, sweeping with his hand for her to enter.

She comes in and he shuts the door. Before she can make her way to her dressing room, he clears his throat and speaks:

'Miss van der Doodle?'

She turns her head, her dazzling blonde locks bouncing on her shoulders. 'Yes?'

'I wonder . . . would you like to—'

He stops and wriggles his left shoulder, frowning. She sees this and looks startled. 'Say, what's up?' she asks, squinting at him.

'I . . . I . . .' he stammers. He wriggles his shoulder some more and his eyes widen, and his moustache twitches.

'Hey, Neddy, you got fleas or something?'

'I . . . I . . .' He tries to speak, but now his shoulder starts moving of its own accord. And then Neddy Noblock starts to titter, then giggle, and then he is laughing, all the while wriggling his shoulder as though a small earthquake is taking place there.

'Hey,' says Bunny, putting her hands on her hips, 'have you been hitting the giggle-juice?'

And then the buttons on the front of Neddy's dinner jacket pop open and out from inside the top of the jacket, near his left shoulder, burst three white doves, their wings a blur as they fly up to the ceiling.

Neddy Noblock is speechless.

Which is more than can be said for Bunny van der Doodle. 'What the deuce are you trying to pull? Ya think that's funny? You little wise guy! Why, I've got a good mind to—'

'Oh dear,' says Neddy. 'I'm so sorry, I have no idea where—'

At that moment, two large white rabbits emerge from inside of the jacket. They jump to the floor and across to Bunny, where they hop about between her high heels.

'Eeeeergh!' she screeches. 'Get 'em away! I'm allergic!'

Neddy is sweating profusely now. He reaches into the jacket pocket, trying to find a handkerchief to mop his brow. He pulls out his hand, and with it a small flag of Botswana. Which is attached to a small flag of Italy. Which is attached to a small flag of New Zealand. Which is attached to a small flag of Iceland. Which is attached to a small flag of China. Which is attached to a small flag of Abyssinia. Which is attached to a small flag of Draddleovstock.

On and on he pulls, and on and on the flags come, until there lies a pile of forty-six flags from various nations at his feet.

Bunny has forgotten about the rabbits and the doves; she is staring incredulously at the livery of the world around Neddy's spats.

Neddy decides to try to grab the rabbits. He reaches out and suddenly, from his sleeves, two enormous bouquets of silk flowers shoot across the room, narrowly avoiding floomp*ing into Bunny's head.*

'Aaaarrrrggghhhh!' *she screams at full volume.*

'Oh, my goodness me,' mutters Neddy, as a long stream of shiny silk handkerchiefs erupts from his breast pocket as though propelled by a missile. And then, when the last of the knotted silks falls to the floor, there is an enormous explosion of confetti that blasts into the air, almost taking Neddy Noblock's nose with it.

All Bunny van der Doodle can do is stare and gasp . . .

. . . as Neddy Noblock looks at us, from all those years ago, and says, 'It was magic I wanted, but not this *kind of magic . . .'*

❃

Harvey Wong had thought that a Saturday night screening of a Wallace Wong feature might help bring Phyllis out of her shell and, he reasoned, what better picture was there, in terms of light-heartedness, than *No Time For Neddy**?

---

* *No Time For Neddy* (Supreme Pictures, 1936). The final known film appearance of Wallace Wong (Conjuror of Wonder!). Wallace Wong gives an effortless performance as Noblock, hinting at how mesmeric he would have been on stage, especially in the final scene where he cannot stop himself from levitating all over the place. *(Information supplied by P.B. Botter, film historian.)*

But as he watched Phyllis sitting there with her dark eyes glazed over and no laughter coming from her (she always laughed, even groaningly, at this picture which she'd seen dozens of times), he realised that *No Time For Neddy* wasn't going to cut it for Phyllis tonight.

'Phyll?' he said over the whirring of the projector and the slightly tinny-sounding dialogue coming from the screen. 'You want to see the rest?'

She stroked Daisy in her lap. 'Thanks, Dad. But not tonight. I'm not really in the mood.'

'That's all right.' He got up and went into the projection room and turned off the projector.

The wall lights in the cinema brightened and he came back out and sat in the chair next to her. 'We can watch Neddy any time,' he said, smiling at his girl.

'Mmm.' She shifted, and Daisy looked up at her, knowing that Phyllis wanted to get up. 'Off you go, Daisy.'

The little terrier sprang gracefully from her lap and waited. Phyllis slowly stood. 'I think I'll go to bed now. G'night.'

'Good night, love.'

She went to leave, but stopped at the door and turned to her father. 'It's because of me that Clement got hurt,' she said, her voice flat. 'He could've been killed because of me.'

'No, Phyllis, that's not—'

'Good night.'

Harvey Wong watched as his daughter and Daisy left the cinema. He listened as she went quietly up the hallway, and heard Daisy's trotting claws on the floorboards where the hall carpet didn't cover the floor. He waited to hear Phyllis open and shut the door to her bedroom.

When he heard her door click, he sat back in the chair and brought his hands together, rubbing his thumbs against each other while he pondered. *She needs something*, he thought. *Something to help her come back. Something special.*

A small smile lifted the corners of his lips. *Her birthday is still nearly six months away . . . but maybe it's time she was given her legacy, a bit early. Maybe that time has arrived.*

Forgotten things

'Come on. This is an early birthday present.'

Phyllis looked up. 'Huh?'

'It's time for me to give you this,' Harvey said. 'Come on, follow me.'

'But it's not my birthday yet . . . Where are we going?'

Her father smiled and said nothing as he left the living room.

'I guess we'd better follow, Daisy.' Phyllis and Daisy went after him, out into the vestibule of their apartment.

'Here,' said Harvey, holding one of her coats out for her to slip her arms into. 'You'll need this. It might be chilly.'

She got into the coat, one arm at a time. 'Where are we going? Siberia?'

Harvey's eyes had a twinkle in them. He bent down, picked up Daisy, tucked her under his arm and opened the front door. 'To the elevator,' he said.

Phyllis pressed the elevator button and they heard the old contraption shudder below before it began its ascent.

Phyllis looked at her father. She raised her eyebrows quizzically. He raised his eyebrows back at her, knowingly, and his smile widened.

The elevator stopped at their floor with a loud, hollow judder. The wooden doors slid open, the stars and comets that were inlaid into one of them disappearing from view as it slid behind the other. Harvey gestured for Phyllis to enter and held the door open as she did. Then he stepped in and the doors closed.

'This is for you, my dear girl,' her father said, reaching into his pocket. He handed her a long silver key.

Phyllis took it. She turned the old-looking key over in her hands. 'Thanks,' she said. 'What's it for?'

Harvey said nothing, but he opened his hand and ran it down the elevator's control panel. When he got to the button for the basement, he pointed with his first finger to the keyhole that was next to the button.

'The basement?' Phyllis asked, puzzled.

'Go on.'

She pushed the key into the hole.

'Turn it once, to the right.'

She did so.

'Now press the button.'

This she did, and the elevator shuddered and began dropping fast—faster than Phyllis had ever known the old crate to travel. She held on tight to the support rail, and Daisy gave a tiny, guttural growl as they all descended.

Phyllis looked out through the window in the elevator doors as they travelled past the next two floors and then on down into the lobby. She saw the gleaming chromium balustrade of the stairs disappear as the elevator took them lower and lower.

Finally, with a huge mechanical groan and a mild jolt, the elevator stopped and the doors slid open with a *whoosh*ing sound and a swirling of dust from the other side.

'Wait in here for one moment,' Harvey Wong said. 'The doors will remain open as long as the key is in. I'll go and turn on some lights.'

He carried Daisy out, and Phyllis peered after them as they disappeared into the darkness. She took a sniff—the air smelt dusty and stale, but sweetly stale, as though it was perfumed with something that had once been fragrant.

'I knew it was here,' Harvey said at last.

Phyllis heard a loud CLICK and suddenly there was light: golden light, emanating from a series of spotlights high up in the ceiling.

'Now you may enter,' said her father.

Phyllis emerged from the elevator onto a small landing which looked out across the entire basement. It was a vast space with a ceiling that must have been at least ten metres high. From the small landing, a staircase led down to the floor below.

Phyllis gasped. Everywhere she looked she saw colour and objects that glittered or sparkled or held the immense possibility of mystery.

'This is all yours, Phyllis,' her father told her. 'The whole lot, and there is no better person to receive this great legacy.'

'This . . . this . . . all of this . . . belonged to *him*?'

Harvey nodded. 'Every prop you see, every item of magic, every illusion and trick and apparatus, was used by your great-grandfather. Happy early birthday, my love.'

Phyllis was so shocked she couldn't speak. Never had she seen such an array of brilliant and beautiful magical objects.

'Come on,' said Harvey, popping Daisy down. 'Let's explore, shall we?'

Phyllis blinked, and Harvey thought he saw a spark of her old light flit across her eyes. 'What a swell idea,' she said as, for the first time in weeks, a smile appeared on her lips.

Harvey led her down the steps into the main basement area. The huge space was crammed with cabinets and brightly decorated boxes and cages and trolleys and props from long, long ago.

Phyllis whistled loudly.

'This way,' her father said, taking her and Daisy up an aisle that snaked between ancient Egyptian sarcophaguses; Hindu sword baskets with dusty silver swords still inserted into the wickerwork; a towering guillotine; a series of tall cabinets with bold zigzags painted all over them; piles of duck pans; enormous botanias of silk and feather flowers that were as tall as Phyllis's waist and wider than five Phyllises standing side-by-side; great mirrored cabinets on wheels; clothes racks hanging with tail coats, Chinese mandarin clothing, sequined female attire, top hats, turbans, pith helmets and jodhpurs and plumed headdresses; and strange, Oriental-looking tea chests stacked high atop one another.

Scattered amongst all of these large props and illusions were beautiful stage tables with black-as-midnight tops and dark crimson velvet drops lined with golden tassels. These magic tables were piled with smaller objects: tubes decorated with stars and moons; deep red and black boxes nested into each other; large silver pans; rubber skulls and other pieces of artificial skeletons; billiard balls arranged in a tall, circular stand; a big card castle, still intact after all this time, with all its thirteen levels of cards looking as if they had just miraculously appeared out of nowhere; and silk handkerchiefs, smaller bouquets of feather flowers, beautiful magic wands of ebony and other exotic dark woods with silver ends, artificial fruits, fake rabbits and rubber doves, copper cups, sparkly red balls and countless other things that Phyllis had only ever read about in her magic magazines.

'There's a lot more in all of those trunks and skips by the far wall,' her father said. 'Some of these things have instructions somewhere . . . you'll have your work cut out for you finding them. Others are . . . well, without instructions or manuals. They're mysteries, I guess. You'll have to work out how they operate. My grandfather wasn't meticulous when it came to recording the ins and outs of all his bits and pieces.'

'I don't mind,' said Phyllis, as Daisy came up to her and made a small gargling sound. 'Look at it all, Daisy,' said Phyllis. 'All of these marvellous things from the days before everything got shrunken down . . . before things became smaller and more ordinary . . .'

Daisy trotted close to Phyllis's ankles, unsure of this strange new world.

They reached a cleared space somewhere in the middle of the basement. Here were some old couches and a few wooden-backed chairs. 'Have a seat,' said Harvey.

Still in shock, Phyllis lowered herself into one of the deep couches. Daisy jumped up next to her and a tiny plume of sweet-smelling dust rose around them.

'Now, some of these things might be dangerous,' Harvey told her. 'I'm trusting you not to take any risks, okay?'

'Sure,' she said.

'Like this one, for example.' He went over to a nearby table where there was a miniature guillotine painted red and gold. 'D'you know what it is?'

Phyllis smiled. 'Oh, Daaad! Of course I do.'

'It's a wrist chopper,' Harvey said, not put off by her response. 'Allow me to demonstrate.'

The apparatus had two holes in the front panel, and a wide blade that lowered when a catch was released. Harvey raised the blade, exposing both the holes. He reached into his pocket and withdrew a thick carrot.

'Do you always carry rabbit food around?' asked Phyllis, smirking.

'Only when I like to prove a point,' he said. 'Or when I think I might meet something furry that hops about and twitches. Now, observe.'

He placed the carrot into one of the holes. Phyllis watched as he pressed the catch. The blade hurtled down with a loud *whooooooosh*, slicing the carrot clean through. One end of the vegetable shot out from the force of the impact and skittered across the floor.

Daisy jumped off the couch and went to look for it.

Phyllis shuddered. She had seen this effect on TV once, and she thought it was okay, but now, seeing it right before her, well . . . there was an added element of danger which made her slightly nervous.

'Now, my turn,' said Harvey. He raised the blade again and set it into position. Then he rolled up the sleeves of his jacket and shirt and placed one of his wrists into one of the holes.

'Dad—' Phyllis was worried that the chopper was so old that it might have become unreliable with disuse.

But Harvey ignored her. With a quick, deft movement, he released the catch—

—and the blade slashed down!

Phyllis had shut her eyes at the crucial moment. When she heard no sound from her father, she gingerly opened one of them.

There he was, his arm extricated from the wrist chopper, hand still intact. He smiled as he wriggled his fingers around.

Phyllis breathed out. 'It still holds up, doesn't it?' she said.

'Still packs a punch, all right. Now you be careful with the sharp things, yes?'

'Promise,' she said.

Suddenly there was a high-pitched yapping and snarling from behind the couch. It was the sort of yapping and snarling Daisy made whenever she was trying to protect Phyllis or her father or Phyllis's friends from danger.

Harvey Wong rushed to where Daisy was crouched low to the ground, her teeth bared, her snout raised at a threatening angle.

Phyllis hopped up and went round to the rear of the couch.

'What is it, Daisy?' asked Harvey.

The terrier had baled something up, something large that was covered with an old sheet. She darted towards it, then back again, then towards it and back, all the while yapping and snarling.

Cautiously, Harvey approached. He took hold of Daisy's collar and drew her to him. Then, crouching, he peered underneath the sheet.

'Goodness me. I'd forgotten about this. She can see the paws,' Mr Wong said, laughing.

He stood, lifting Daisy, and then he whipped the sheet away.

Daisy yapped even louder and wriggled, trying to get free.

Phyllis's jaw dropped open.

Standing there in front of them was a life-size Bengal tiger, about to pad towards them. Its eyes glinted and its huge teeth were bared.

'Wow!' Phyllis loved it straightaway.

'Watch this,' Harvey said. He handed Daisy (still wriggling, but a bit calmer now that she could sense no panic in either Phyllis or her father) to Phyllis. Then he went to a table by the tiger's haunches and took up a small oblong-shaped box. He moved a lever on the box and, silently, the tiger began walking towards them, its head lowering and rising, its tail swishing ever so slightly.

Harvey moved the lever back to where it had been and the tiger stopped.

'That's beautiful,' said Phyllis, beaming. 'That's absolutely *beeeeyuuuutiful*!'

'That's yours as well,' said her dad.

And then Phyllis saw something that made her gasp as though the breath had been knocked out of her. 'Dad! What's happened to the wall? How come . . . but we're *underground* . . . how can that—?'

Harvey laughed as he watched his daughter's incredulous expression. She was staring at the space beyond the tiger, at a place where the basement should have been defined by a stone wall, like the other stone walls that hemmed in the area.

But, instead of a wall, there was a view of a bright, sunshine-filled harbour with sparkling blue water and ships and wharves and buildings in the far distance.

'No, love. It's not real. It's a backdrop.'

'It can't be.' She put Daisy down and went up to it. 'I can see the water rippling . . . it's so—' Then she stopped. 'Why, so it is!'

Now that she was closer to it, Phyllis could see that it was a little mildewed and that it was, indeed, a backdrop painted as realistically as could ever be achieved.

'New York City harbour,' said her father. 'Wallace Wong used it in 1926. Notice something missing?'

Phyllis stepped back and scanned the entire canvas. She looked carefully. Then she said, 'The Statue of Liberty!'

'And that's what he made disappear.'

Phyllis looked at him in wonder.

'Oh, it was one of his finest moments, Phyll. He had an enormous seating area erected on the foreshore so the audience could see the actual harbour—' he swept his hand across the backdrop —'this very scene, but with the Statue of Liberty in its proper place. He even arranged, at considerable expense, to have the identical boats you see on the backdrop here moored in the actual harbour at the time of his performance. He had a huge arch built on his stage with a curtain that would fall quickly down and could then be raised just as swiftly.'

'I get it,' said Phyllis, her eyes shining. 'And the backdrop was behind the curtain, yes? It would fall down with it?'

'Exactly. He announced that he was going to vanish the statue. He called for quiet. He said his magic word, then PRESTO!—the curtain dropped! Three seconds later, when the backdrop was settled, the curtain was pulled up again. And there, seemingly, was New York harbour, minus its most famous inhabitant!'

Phyllis shook her head. She felt light, almost giddy, at the marvellous audacity of the illusion.

Harvey admired the backdrop. 'Wallace paid for the best scenery artist the theatre had ever known to do that. It cost him a small fortune, but I do believe he got his money's worth.'

'I'll say.' Phyllis turned and surveyed the wonders that filled her new place. Wonders that she had only barely dreamt about whenever she had imagined what magic would have been like in her great-grandfather's day.

'Dad?'

'Yes, Phyll?'

'Thanks.'

'Happy early birthday.' He gave her a hug. 'And welcome back, my girl. Welcome back.'

Illusionations

For nearly all of the next week, Phyllis spent most of her spare time down in the basement—*her* basement—immersing herself in the almost-forgotten illusions and tricks of her great-grandfather.

Her father got the furnace working for her; the long winter afternoons and evenings had now reached their full chill factor, and because of its subterranean stone walls, the basement was much colder than their apartment, and even colder than the street outside. The furnace was a big monster and still worked well, so with her scarf on and a heavy coat, Phyllis wasn't bothered by the crispness down there. Nor was Daisy, who spent most of her time wearing one of her own little coats (a smart tartan number Harvey had bought for her in London), curled up in a corner of the couch with one eye on Phyllis as she pottered about and explored the many treasures.

One evening, as Phyllis was pondering the intricacies and workings of an especially large set of five gleaming linking rings, she said to her little friend, 'It's just like Mrs L. always says, Daisy. Everything from the past has its own story to tell. Where d'you think old Wallace might've performed with these? Shanghai? Cairo? Istanbul? Paris? I wonder if we will ever know.'

Daisy lifted her snout from her paws and cocked her head to one side. Then she licked her lips and settled herself back into her half-slumber.

It got to the point where Phyllis was spending so much time in the basement that Harvey started bringing her dinners down on a serving trolley. He didn't mind doing that—whenever he found her, her eyes were always gleaming and a smile was never far from her lips. He did, however, draw the line when she asked if she could sleep down there. He insisted that her bed was a much better place, and that it was a good idea not to become totally obsessed with her treasures.

Clement wondered where she disappeared to every day. They hadn't been hanging out after school at all. When Clement texted her to see if she wanted to do something after she had arrived home, more often than not she had left her phone upstairs.

She hadn't told Clement about the basement; she felt that, just for the present, she wanted to keep it all to herself. Maybe until she knew exactly what was there, and until she felt she had the knowledge of it all. Phyllis knew that there would come a time—the right time—when she could share everything with her best (human) friend.

Clement, though a little puzzled, resigned himself to afternoons of half-hearted homework, even more half-hearted xylophone practice and furtive hours in his room, battling against unimaginably evil zombie accountants who wanted to simultaneously take over the known universe and balance the account books of enormous financial corporations.

Late one Saturday afternoon, amongst all the flip-over boxes, the phantom cabinets, the card ladders, the 'spiderweb hemispheres of mystery', the long, oblong boxes—beautifully painted with blazing blue and silver starbursts—in which you could put people before sawing them in half, late one Saturday afternoon, amongst all these wonders, Phyllis found an object that made her stop in her tracks.

In a far corner, hidden beneath a dusty canvas dropsheet, was a trunk. As soon as Phyllis had taken off the dropsheet and seen the trunk, she knew exactly what it was.

And every pore in her body tingled as if an electric current had suddenly ZINGed straight through her.

'Daisy,' she whispered. 'Look! It's his Houdini substitution trunk. It's the trunk he went into in 1936, and never reappeared from. This was the last place that Wallace Wong, Conjuror of Wonder!, was ever seen!'

The realisation made her dizzy; she reached out and put both hands on top of the trunk to steady herself.

Daisy sniffed all around the trunk's corners.

Phyllis took a few deep breaths. She stood straight and, her fingers trembling, lifted the three catches on the lid. Slowly, for it was not light, she raised the lid of the trunk.

A musty smell wafted up. To Phyllis it smelt of age and faraway places. She set the lid upright and peered into the rich green lining inside.

She had to look very hard to detect the method of escape, but she eventually found it. She ran her hand gently along the lining, her eyes wide, her breath shallow.

Then she gasped. In the bottom of the trunk, written onto the dark green lining in a lighter green ink, was a series of numbers and symbols interspersed here and there with small, strange drawings, the likes of which Phyllis had never seen.

She looked at the numerals and the writing, trying to work out what it meant. She went and found her notepad, in which she'd been making notes about the workings of the tricks she'd been discovering. Carefully she transcribed the numbers and the symbols and the small drawings, exactly as they appeared in the bottom of the trunk.

She stared at what she had written, and she shook her head. It made no sense. She looked back into the trunk and her gaze travelled along the numbers, symbols and drawings once again.

And she saw something else.

Tucked into a corner of the trunk, in a spot where the lining had come partially loose and was rucked up, there was an object. A small sphere.

Phyllis held her breath. She reached in and picked up the ball.

Her eyes grew wide as she beheld it in the palm of her hand. It seemed to be made of glass and for its size was quite heavy. It fitted neatly into her hand. She curled her fingers around it and rolled her hand over—it was comfortable to palm.

She turned her hand over again and opened her fingers. She moved the sphere around, letting the lights from above shine into it.

And she gasped.

Inside she saw brightness: gold, red, purple and white tendrils of colour that swirled deep into the glass ball. They all merged in a point; at a place in the bottom of the sphere that looked like it was a long way from where Phyllis was standing.

She turned the glass ball slowly. The swirls of colour sparkled, and they appeared to go deeper, corkscrewing away towards a never-ending point into the depths of the sphere.

Phyllis was mesmerised.

She was still staring at it hours later when her father came and fetched her to come upstairs for bed.

She spent the next day exploring the contents of the many skips and trunks and chests in which lots of the smaller props were stored. Here she had found beautifully decorated boxes and pans and tubes, many painted with Oriental scenes in the Japanese style of the 1920s. The antique-looking pictures captured her imagination straightaway.

She began inspecting the boxes and tubes and cylinders, and was delighted to find that many of them contained ingeniously concealed secrets: platforms that moved up and down; hidden flaps that swung away; sliding doors in the backs or false bottoms that could only be released when you held your finger on the cleverly disguised button or catch. She marvelled at these props, and the way they operated silently and swiftly, almost in the blink of an eye.

This was a sort of cunning design she had never imagined. The cleverness and the sheer *audacity* of the thinking that had created these props made her heart quiver.

And something inside her stirred, some fragment in a pattern that was reaching out to her from long ago, from her past even before she had been born . . .

❃

The fragment reached out to her fully that night as she lay sleeping. The pattern emerged clearly into her mind, through the silent wisps of her dreams, and Phyllis woke up with a gasp.

Daisy, curled into her on top of the blankets, stood and shook herself until her ears flapped. She peered into Phyllis's face.

Phyllis sat up. Even though there was no light on in her room, everything was bright. She felt like she could see through everything around her—darkness, unspoken words, even time.

'Daisy! All those things! I know!'

Daisy cocked her head and licked Phyllis's hand.

'I know how he did it. And I know how to prove it!'

Daisy blinked her big brown eyes, listening.

'We're going to put on a show!' Phyllis told her. 'A show that'll lift the lid on it all. Frock-coat guy won't know what's hit him!'

The show goes on

'My heavens,' said Mrs Lowerblast as she and Minette Bulbolos entered the Wallace Wong cinema for the first time.

'This way, please, ladies,' said Harvey Wong, leading them to the deep chairs in the front row. 'Best seats in the house, for two very special friends of my daughter's.'

'Ooooh,' breathed Minette, getting a heavily eyelashed eyeful of the beautiful decorations. 'How long has this been here?'

'As long as the building itself,' said Harvey. 'It's our little oasis where we can escape into the past every now and then.'

Mrs Lowerblast eased herself down into the chair, her head swivelling all around. 'It is *wunderbar*!' she exclaimed as she arranged her mauve scarf around her shoulders. 'Divine, *ja*. Purely divine!'

Harvey pointed to the black velvet drapes before them. In front of the drapes, on the same black velvet that also lined the floor, stood five empty black-topped tables with bamboo legs and deep crimson velvet drops lined with golden braiding. 'We don't normally have that curtain there,' Harvey said. 'Or the black carpet. Phyllis has redecorated for tonight's performance.'

'I was very happy to get her invitation,' said Minette. 'I was missing her.'

'As were we all,' said Mrs Lowerblast. 'Tell me, Mr Wong: how is Phyllis faring?'

'She has returned,' answered Harvey.

Minette smiled.

Harvey looked towards the hallway. 'If you'll excuse me, I think that was the doorbell.' He bowed his head and left them.

'Such splendor,' Mrs Lowerblast said. 'It reminds me of a theatre I used to attend when I was a girl back in Berlin. *Fati* used to take me there often.'

'I'd certainly rather play in a house like this than some of the flea-bitten dives I get booked into,' said Minette. 'A girl feels classy just *looking* at this décor.'

'Through here,' came Harvey's voice from up the hallway.

'I wonder who else is coming,' Mrs Lowerblast said.

'Thank you, Mr Wong,' came Chief Inspector Inglis's voice.

Minette quickly arranged her hair and straightened her blouse to its best advantage.

Harvey led Barry, and behind him, Clement on his crutches, into the cinema.

'Wow!' Clement gasped when he saw the richness before him. 'Phyll's told me about this place, but I just thought it'd be a wall screen with some speakers and beanbags or something. This is like . . . like . . .' He pushed his glasses further up his nose. 'I dunno *what* it's like.'

'Please, have a seat,' Harvey said to Clement and the Inspector.

'Good evening, Mrs Lowerblast,' Barry Inglis greeted her.

'*Guten abend*, Chief Inspector.'

'Good evening, Miss Bulbolos.'

Minette turned in her chair and flashed him a wide, perfect smile. 'Hello again. Long time, no see?'

'Duty,' Barry said, nodding. 'No rest for the wicked-watchers. I've come straight from the job now, as a matter of fact.'

'Ah. That explains that fetching suit.' Minette spied Clement sliding into the chair next to the Inspector's. 'Hello, Mr Xylophones! How's that leg?'

'Um . . . er . . . hi,' Clement managed to get out before his cheeks flushed brightly. 'Erm . . . healing quickly . . . the doctor says.'

Minette beamed at him, and he fidgeted in his seat.

Harvey had made his way down to the small stage area, with Daisy draped across his arms. 'Ladies and gentlemen,' he announced, 'I cannot tell you how much pleasure it gives me to welcome you all here this evening. My daughter has prepared a show for you. I do not know what she is about to present, for she has kept it under wraps, even from me. But, knowing Phyllis, I have no hesitation in predicting that what you are about to see will be both brilliant and astonishing. She has never been anything less.'

If smiles had sounds, the auditorium would have been humming.

'And now, may I present, for the first time in the Wallace Wong cinema, Miss Phyllis Wong and her Illusionations!'

There was an enthusiastic round of applause as Harvey took Daisy up the aisle and into the projection booth. Slowly the house lights dimmed and the electrical stars began to glow overhead.

'Oh, the heavens,' said Mrs Lowerblast, looking up. 'Sparkle-*acious*!'

Clement pushed his head back into the chair and pushed his glasses further up his nose as the artificial galaxy came softly and twinklingly to life.

Then the blackened stage area was gradually illuminated and music started up from somewhere behind the curtain: a high-pitched and sweetly haunting tune. To Minette, it sounded like it was being played by spirits or beings not from this realm, and she shivered as her shoulders were quickly riddled with goosebumps.

Mrs Lowerblast gasped. 'Ach!'

On the stage, a beautiful, big red Chinese fan unfolded out of the blackness, suspended by nothing but the air around it. The fan opened out to become almost a metre wide. It hung there, quivering in the air. Then it shook and sailed down to the floor, where it rested against one of the tables.

'Where did it come from?' Mrs Lowerblast whispered. 'It . . . it just . . . materialised from nowhere!'

Chief Inspector Inglis cocked his head as he watched what happened next. A wide, flat box decorated with beautifully painted scenes of old China became visible, floating high across the stage. The box hovered, as though carried by invisible phantoms, before lowering onto one of the tables.

And then, when it was lowered, all at once there appeared, out of nowhere, a shallow copper bowl sitting on the table beside it.

Minette's goosebumps had spread beyond her shoulders, and she squirmed in her seat.

Clement's mouth was open. He tried to see if there were any wires or strings, but he couldn't detect a thing.

Now, on the stage, a single billiard ball, bright red and shining, popped into view, suspended in the air. It floated across the stage, hovered for a moment and then, as the high-pitched music grew louder and more ghostly, a tall piece of apparatus, similar to a round clock face on a short pedestal, manifested upon another table. One moment the table was empty, the next the apparatus was there! The floating billiard ball glided down into a hole in the edge of the circular face of the apparatus and settled there.

On the other side of the stage, another red billiard ball appeared, floating more than a metre from the floor. It, too, travelled across the stage and then settled into another of the holes in the apparatus. It was followed by another billiard ball, and then another, and another four after that, all of them popping into existence from an unknown place, and all of them floating across the stage and settling into the remaining holes in the round face of the apparatus.

The Chief Inspector's eyes narrowed. He knew Phyllis was clever; he had never doubted that from the first time he had met her. *But*, he wondered, *what cleverness was abounding tonight?*

Now a fan of cards popped into view high in the air, a full deck spread out in an elegant arc. Next to it another fan of cards appeared, and then the first lot closed and vanished, and the second deck copied the first. It all happened to the high-pitched notes wafting through the darkness.

Harvey Wong, sitting with Daisy in a chair at the back of the auditorium, glowed with pleasure and pride.

And then, as the music seemed to be reaching a crescendo, on the remaining empty table, several objects miraculously materialised from nowhere, including a tall green box decorated with images of peacocks and vases full of orchids and, next to that, a bright red cube-shaped tube, smaller than the green peacock box and embellished with scenes of Chinese village life from long ago.

Now the music hung on a single note, stretching out as if it could distort all of time. Everyone watched as, from behind one of the tables, a long roll of what appeared to be bright yellow silk emerged. The rolled-up silk rose into the air, higher and higher and then, with the smallest of *whoosh*es, the bulk of the silk dropped to the ground, with the top part of it still suspended.

The high note grew louder and vibrated on the air. The screen of yellow silk billowed and trembled. And then—*suddenly*!—all of the yellow silk dropped to the floor to reveal Phyllis Wong standing centre-stage, dressed in a flowing red dress of the Oriental style popular in the 1920s.

'Good lord!' Inspector Inglis exclaimed. He began clapping without realising it.

Mrs Lowerblast, Minette and Harvey swelled the applause, while Clement tried unsuccessfully to blow a few loud whistles through his teeth. Daisy barked appreciatively.

Phyllis smiled and bowed. Then she stepped forward and said, 'Ladies and gentlemen and Daisy, I would like to present for you tonight some magic that has not been seen for a very long time. It was performed by my great-grandfather Wallace Wong, Conjuror of Wonder! And now it's my magic.'

The audience settled deeper into their plush chairs, and a sense of great excitement rippled through the cinema.

Phyllis's smile widened and became inscrutable, hinting that she knew vast and strange secrets, but she was only going to share a small sliver of those secrets with her assembled guests. She straightened herself so that she seemed even taller than she usually was and spread the fingers of both hands wide in front of her.

The lights changed to a pale greenish glow, as Phyllis went to the billiard-ball stand. She withdrew one of the balls and held it in front of her face. Then, with a flick of her wrist, she tossed it into the air above her.

And it vanished completely!

There were gasps. Clement shook his head. He never knew she could do this.

Phyllis saw Clement shaking his head and she gave him a big grin and a wink. Then she took a second ball from the apparatus. She held it at shoulder level to her body, her arm outstretched. Quickly she turned her hand over, and back again. The ball was gone.

She picked out the next five billiard balls and, with astonishing speed, she tossed them and turned them and drew her hands across them. Every one of them dissolved into nothing.

There was one ball left. Phyllis took it from the stand and held it between her thumb and first finger. She raised her hand and extended her middle finger. Another billiard ball appeared, next to the first, nestled between her first and middle finger! She extended her next finger—a third ball popped into view! She stretched her little finger out, and a fourth ball was there!

She raised her other, empty, hand. With a quick flicking gesture a green billiard ball appeared between her thumb and first finger. Then a yellow ball was between her next two fingers. Then an orange one, and a bright purple one (Mrs Lowerblast nodded approvingly at that one).

With both hands fully splayed and filled with billiard balls, Phyllis opened her arms wide, gave a short, sharp flick of her wrists, and all the billiard balls were gone, replaced instantaneously by two enormous bouquets of bright, feathery flowers.

The house erupted with applause.

'Thank you, my friends,' Phyllis said when the applause had faded. She placed the bouquets on one of the empty tables and picked up a large blue-and-white ceramic bowl. She moved downstage and placed the bowl on the floor in front of the table upon which the flat box with the scenes of old China painted on it and the copper bowl rested.

At the same time she pressed a button on her iPod (hidden in the waistband of her red dress) and a lilting Chinese tune began to waft into the cinema.

'Behold,' she announced. 'The Mysterious Bowl of Transformation!'

She picked up the box and removed its lid. With a sweeping gesture, she showed the box to be full of brightly coloured confetti. She placed the box and lid back on the table and took up the copper bowl. Carefully she took out handfuls of confetti from the box and filled the bowl. A few pieces of confetti spilled out and floated slowly down to the black floor.

When she had filled the copper bowl to the brim, Phyllis went back to the table and placed it down behind the box. She picked up the box and then its lid, put the lid on the box, and set it aside on a smaller side table by her elbow. From this table she picked up a long, crimson silk scarf, which she draped around her neck.

She took the copper bowl and walked closer to the audience, holding the bowl at shoulder-height. When she was in front of Minette, Phyllis blew a little, and some of the confetti wafted out of the copper bowl, showering Minette's hair.

'Ah,' Minette laughed. 'It's probably the closest I'll ever get to having confetti thrown on me!'

Phyllis smiled her inscrutable smile. Then she took the crimson silk from around her neck and, holding the bowl on the palm of one hand, she draped the silk over the bowl so that it covered it and her hand completely.

She stood still for a moment, perfectly motionless, before she passed her long fingers across the top of the silk. In a flash, she whipped the silk from the bowl and presented the bowl to the audience.

The confetti was nowhere to be seen, not a scrap. Instead, the copper bowl was filled to the brim with water!

'Wow!' said Clement, and everyone applauded as Phyllis went and poured the water out into the blue-and-white ceramic bowl on the floor.

Phyllis put the empty copper bowl aside and crossed to the table with the tall green peacock box and the bright red cube-shaped tube.

'And now,' she said, her voice low and commanding, 'a rarely seen moment of mystery!'

She opened the lid at the top of the peacock box and reached inside to withdraw two things: an orange cube-shaped box adorned with birds of paradise and other exotic creatures of the air, and a vivid yellow silk handkerchief. She placed the handkerchief over her arm and held up the orange box.

'In olden days people would keep their valuables in special jewel chests, similar to this one. It was a safe place to keep them and, what's more, a person could take the box with them when they travelled.'

She lifted the hinged lid of the orange box and brought it forward for the audience to inspect.

Mrs Lowerblast and Minette peered into the dark blue velvet lining. 'Very swish,' Minette commented.

'I wonder,' Phyllis said, 'whether one of the gentlemen in the audience would be so kind as to lend me an item of value? Say, a wristwatch?'

Clement frowned—he did not own such a thing. He always used his phone (if he hadn't misplaced it) to tell the time.

Chief Inspector Inglis looked a little nervous. 'Erm . . . well, you're not going to smash it up, are you?' he asked. 'I once saw a magician do that on television and it got a bit ugly.'

'You can trust me, sir.' She smiled at him and he knew he had no choice.

'Yes. Of course I can. Hmm.' He didn't sound entirely happy about the situation, but he unclasped the large silver band, slipped the watch off his wrist and held it out.

'Please place it into the jewel chest,' said Phyllis.

The Inspector did so.

'Now close the lid.'

Once again, Barry obeyed.

'Thank you.' Phyllis went back to the table and placed the orange box down and moved the larger peacock box out of the way so that the audience would have an unobstructed view.

'But,' she continued, 'it was a sad fact of life in olden days that bandits were at work. Things haven't really changed, have they, Chief Inspector?'

'That they certainly haven't, Miss Wong.'

'It's probably for the best,' said Minette, fluttering her eyelashes at him. 'Otherwise you wouldn't have a job.'

'Hmm,' hmmed Barry Inglis.

Phyllis smiled. 'There was, however, a clever conjuror in ancient China. A man who solved the problem. He invented a special tube, just like this one . . .' She picked up the small tube, which was roughly the same dimension as the orange box in which the Inspector's watch had been placed. 'If there were bandits about, well . . . allow me to demonstrate.'

She took the orange box and slid it gently into the open-ended red tube. It was a snug fit. Then she pulled the silk handkerchief from her arm and covered the tube and the orange box. She held the covered objects on the palm of her left hand.

'If a bandit struck on the highway, behold!'

She held the handkerchief and the tube by one of its corners. Then she thrust her other hand down, spearing it clean through one end of the tube and pulling the silk handkerchief cleanly out of the other end.

The orange box had completely vanished!

Phyllis withdrew her hand from the tube and held it up, looking at her audience through the open ends.

'Whoah!' said the Inspector, his stomach feeling fluttery. He squinted. 'Where's my property?'

Phyllis's eyes gleamed (this was one of the best parts about magic for her—*she had them*!). 'You see,' she said, 'the conjuror made the tube so that, if any danger threatened, one merely had to insert the jewel chest into it and—presto!—the jewel chest would be spirited back to the owner's home!'

She went back to the table, picked up the large green peacock box and opened the lid. From within she produced the orange jewel chest.

'Ah!' gasped Mrs Lowerblast.

Phyllis brought the jewel chest over to Barry. 'Open it, if you would be so kind, sir.'

Chief Inspector Inglis looked at her, and his lips almost curled at the edges. He slowly lifted the lid of the orange box and reached inside.

'Well, I'll be cuffed,' he said as he took his watch from inside the box.

'Awesome!' said Clement, and the applause came again.

Phyllis went back to the stage and performed one final feat: she took a small piece of tissue paper, about fifteen centimetres long by two centimetres wide, and tore it into small squares. She held the wad of squares together and dipped them into the ceramic bowl of water until they were soaked. Then she took up the big red fan, held the sopping wad of tissue in her hand, and proceeded to waft the fan across the wet tissue.

Slowly, rising silently into the air, hundreds of tiny pieces of white tissue paper floated. Phyllis kept fanning, and the white squares of dry paper kept appearing, on and on and on, hundreds and hundreds and maybe even thousands, for they kept coming, wafting and billowing all across the stage and into the audience and settling upon her friends and the chairs and Daisy like the most gentle and beautiful of snowbursts.

'The Miraculous Snowstorm of Huangshan,' Phyllis said happily. 'And that, my friends, is the end of my performance!'

Briefing the Chief Inspector

When Phyllis's performance had concluded, Harvey invited the guests into the living room, where a small supper of cakes, soft drinks and champagne had been laid out.

Before Chief Inspector Inglis left the cinema, Phyllis took him to one side and said to her father, 'We'll be out soon. There's something I have to talk to the Inspector about. In private.'

'Okay,' said Harvey. 'I'll make sure Clement doesn't polish off all the cakes.'

When he had gone, the Inspector said, 'Well, Miss Wong, I have to say, you were a knockout. I have no idea how you accomplished any of those effects. And I noted the touch of theremin music that played at the beginning. It sent phantoms swirling all about me!'

'You knew that was a theremin?' Phyllis asked, impressed.

'Ah. I have a slight musical background. From a misspent youth, some might say. Now, what do you have to tell me?'

'Have a seat,' said Phyllis. 'This is big.'

The Chief Inspector raised his eyebrows and went and sat in the front row chair that Minette Bulbolos had occupied. He clasped his hands in his lap and looked at Phyllis with the expression he used whenever he was about to hear an important confession from a suspect.

'I know exactly how frock-coat guy stole the blue wren bookend and the Van Rockechild diamonds,' Phyllis announced. 'And I'm going to show you how he did it.'

Slowly, the Inspector's thumbs came to attention. Then they went horizontal and began twiddling around each other.

Phyllis took a deep breath as she stood centre-stage. 'Chief Inspector, I'm about to break the code of all magicians worldwide. I'm going to show you how some of these tricks were done. It's the last thing I've ever wanted to do, to reveal the secrets, but I have to do it to prove these things to you. Chief Inspector, you must give me your solemn word—you must swear to me—that you will never—*never*—reveal to anyone what I am about to tell and show you.'

The Inspector stopped twiddling. He nodded. 'I give you my word,' he said solemnly.

'Cross your aorta nineteen different ways?'

The Inspector blinked. 'Erm . . . yes . . . yes . . . I do.'

Phyllis raised an eyebrow at him.

'Oh, all right.' He unclasped his hands, extended his right hand's index finger and ran it in a crazy star-shaped pattern over his breast pocket. 'Is that right?'

'Good,' she said. 'Now, watch closely.'

She went to the table upon which the box embellished with scenes of old China and the copper bowl that had been filled with water were placed.

'The Mysterious Bowl of Transformation is indeed *very* mysterious,' she told him. 'And ingenious. It's a very old effect, no longer performed much these days.' She looked at him and smiled. 'What did you like best about it, Chief Inspector?'

'Hmm. Well, that's easy. When the confetti disappeared and the water had filled the bowl in its place.'

'And where did the confetti go to and the water come from?'

'I am totally in the dark about that. I have no idea how all that liquid could have come from nowhere.'

'Watch.'

She slid the box forward, picked it up, moved her hand behind it and stepped back.

The Inspector gasped. There on the table, sitting next to the copper bowl, was another identical copper bowl, filled with confetti. 'Ah! There were two bowls!'

'That's right,' said Phyllis.

Barry Inglis frowned and rubbed his chin. 'But how . . . ? I mean, we only saw *one* bowl!'

'No, you saw both bowls. But not when you thought you did.'

Barry remained silent. He looked at her, waiting.

'I used some misdirection,' Phyllis said. 'That, and a cleverly gimmicked prop. I'll show you.'

She brought the box over to him and turned it around so that he could see the back of it.

The Chief Inspector shook his head slowly. 'I would've never imagined,' he said softly.

'See? The back of it is cut away. From the front it looks like a complete box, but not from the back. And inside—well, look.'

She put one hand underneath the box and gently pushed. The bottom of the box, lined in black felt, moved silently upwards.

'It has a moveable bottom. It goes up and down, sort of like an elevator, when the box is raised or lowered, depending on whether there's anything underneath it.'

'Ingenious,' said the Chief Inspector.

'What happened was this: I had the second bowl—the one filled with water—already positioned on the table, under the box. I filled the other bowl with the confetti—'

'—Hang on, how did you get the confetti out of a box that has no real bottom? Wouldn't it have spilled out as soon as you picked the box up from the table?'

'That's the other secret of the box. Look.' Phyllis removed the lid to show the leftover confetti inside the top of the box. 'Put your hand in,' she said to Barry.

He did so. His fingers didn't go down far at all. 'Ah! A shallow top.'

'Exactly. Just deep enough to contain a small amount of confetti, while giving the appearance that the whole box is filled with it.'

Barry nodded. 'Go on.'

'Well, I filled the first bowl with confetti. Then I put the lid back on the box, which, as you recall, had been sitting in the same spot up to this point in the trick. Now the next step is the true bit of brilliance. The substitution. I had the confetti bowl in my left hand and I brought it over to the box, and put it down on the table, behind the box.'

'Yes. I witnessed that.'

'As I did that, I picked up the box in my other hand and moved it away. And you saw the confetti bowl on the table, where I'd put it.'

'Yes . . .'

'But it wasn't. It was the water-filled bowl, with a round sheet of plastic on top, and on top of that round sheet of plastic there was a thin layer of confetti that had been stuck down. So that bowl looked like the confetti bowl.'

Barry Inglis scratched his chin. 'Huh?'

'You thought you saw me put the confetti bowl down as I moved the box. What I actually did was this: I put it quickly down behind the box on the table, smacking it against the table so that you heard it being placed there. But I never let go of the bowl. Then I lifted the box, and at the same time I lifted the confetti bowl, carefully keeping the confetti bowl hidden behind the box. As I lifted the box, the elevator-bottom-flap dropped down and I slid the confetti bowl into the compartment made by the moveable flap within the box. As I raised the box, you saw the other bowl—the one filled with water, with the confetti gimmick on the top—on the table. Because of where it was, it appeared to be the same bowl I had just supposedly set down.'

'Good lord. I could've sworn it was the same bowl. I mean, you just put it down and moved the box . . .'

Phyllis smiled. Even though it pained her to be revealing the secret, she couldn't think of a better person to have to reveal it to.

'Then,' she continued, 'all I had to do was drape the silk over the water bowl and remove it again, at the same time pulling away the round plastic confetti gimmick which has a small looped wire on it to grip it by. I put the silk—with the confetti gimmick hidden under it—on the table, poured out the water and that was that!'

'That's amazing,' said the Inspector. 'So clever. So many things to think of.'

Phyllis crossed the stage to the table on which sat the tall green peacock box, the bright red cube-shaped tube, the orange cube-shaped box and the yellow silk handkerchief. 'This trick used the same substitution principle for part of it.' She picked up the tall green box and brought it across to the Inspector. 'See?' She turned it around and he saw that it also had a cut-away back.

Phyllis put her hand under it and pushed up. 'Once again, this box has an elevator bottom.

I used two orange boxes here: one already contained in this box, and the other one, the one you put your watch into.'

'Ah,' said Barry. 'And you did the switcheroo in the same way?'

'Similar,' Phyllis said. 'I pretended to put the orange box down onto the table behind this larger one, and I lifted the larger one as I slid the orange box into it, revealing the second orange box in place of the original one on the table.'

'Hey, wait just a second! I saw the orange box completely vanish when you put it in that tube. You shoved the handkerchief all the way through, for crying out loud. How did you do *that*?'

Phyllis gave her inscrutable smile, and the Inspector knew, even before she opened her mouth to speak, that he wasn't going to get the answer.

'That part of the trick,' she said to him, 'isn't important for us. You don't need to know about that. It doesn't have anything to do with frock-coat guy and his crimes.'

The Inspector sank back a little in his chair. He felt it would be useless to try any further with this line of enquiry.

Phyllis swept her hand across the stage. 'Chief Inspector, this is how frock-coat guy stole the blue wren bookend from Mrs L.,' she said, her eyes bright. 'Going on everything she told us, there's no other way.'

The Chief Inspector listened to her. He saw the intensity in her gaze. He heard the conviction in her voice. At that moment, he knew that she had a mind unlike any other he had encountered in all his time on the force.

Phyllis went on: 'Frock-coat guy would've made his bag just like these boxes, with a cut-away back and an elevator-sliding-bottom. The only difference would've been that he made his bag with a real bottom in it, one that can separate in the middle and slide up against the inner sides of the bag without hindering the movement of the elevator flap. That way he could come in with the fake blue wren bookend—the one he'd made—already concealed inside the bag. He put the bag on the counter, the real bottom slid up against the insides of the bag, and the fake bookend was sitting there on the counter. Then, he examined the genuine bookend, put it down with a light bang on the counter so that Mrs L. heard it making contact, picked up the bag while holding the real bookend behind it and slid the real bookend into the elevator-flap compartment in the bag. All he had to do was put the bag down on the floor, and Mrs L. was none the wiser.

There was the bookend still sitting in front of her on the counter, the one she thought was genuine!'

Barry let out an enormous breath. 'And there's the wonder of it!' he exclaimed. 'I'm glad Marlene Parry isn't hearing this.'

Phyllis frowned. 'Don't you believe me?' she asked in a wounded voice.

The Inspector leant forward. 'I believe every word you have told me. I believe you have cracked it, Miss Wong. No, it's just that people like Marlene Parry would never accept explanations that are so far . . . so far *out of the ordinary*. She wouldn't be able to get her head around it.'

Phyllis smiled at him. 'Sometimes extraordinary things come along, and they shake everything up. And things are never the same again.'

'And ain't that the truth,' said Chief Inspector Inglis.

'And I know how he got the necklace too,' Phyllis said.

Barry shook his head. He was feeling a little dizzy. 'Go on,' he said. 'Tell me.'

'No. I'll show you. Just shut your eyes for a minute.'

Chief Inspector Barry Inglis of the Fine Arts and Antiques Squad of the Metropolitan Police shut his eyes.

'No peeping.'

'I am not a man who peeps, Miss Wong.'

A minute passed, then another. Then Barry Inglis heard Phyllis say, as if from a great distance, 'Okay, you can look now.'

He opened his eyes. Phyllis was nowhere to be seen. He stared at the black stage and suddenly he heard the theremin music—the high, wailing melody—filling the cinema.

He sat there, waiting. The music wafted around him like a cobweb. He felt a shiver running down his spine and he did his best not to shudder. He had always found the theremin to be an unnerving instrument, although he had never admitted it to anyone.

A few moments passed. He looked around nervously. He was just about to call out to Phyllis when, in a blink, the large red fan swept itself up off the floor and hovered high in the air.

The Inspector blinked at the abruptness of it.

The fan closed a little, opened again, closed some more, and opened fully. And then it fluttered, like a hesitant bird, before swooping down and forwards and straight at the Chief Inspector in his chair!

Instinctively, he closed his eyes, brought his knees up, flung his arms across his head, and tried to curl up into the smallest ball he could manage. Which wasn't very small at all, for he was a tallish man.

Nothing happened. There was only the haunting strains of the theremin, giving him the mild willies.

He took his arms from his head and opened his eyes, lowering his feet back to the floor. There was the red fan, hovering in front of and slightly above him.

It fluttered silently and then . . .

. . . *it vanished!*

The Inspector gasped loudly. He looked around. There was no sign of the big red fan anywhere.

The music faded away and a voice came from the darkness in front of him. 'Had you there, didn't I, Chief Inspector?'

Barry's eyes grew wide as he beheld Phyllis Wong slowly appearing out of the blackness. First her head, then the shoulders of her red dress, then her arms and then the rest of her all manifested before him.

'Good lord,' he said softly. 'You were there all the time?'

'Camouflaged in the blackness,' she said, smiling. She held up the dark black velvet cloak with sleeves that she had been wearing. 'This is made of exactly the same velvet as the backdrop and the stuff I laid down on the floor. It's an old principle in magic.'

'Go on,' said Barry.

'When you have a dark, dense area, it absorbs light, and therefore there won't be any shadows. So all the blackness ends up merging together. I was wearing this—' she threw the cloak at him, and he caught it—'and, when I stood against the backdrop, I was invisible. So anything I moved appeared to move by itself. And producing things was easy.' She reached down to the floor and plucked something up. It was only when she held it against her red dress that Barry could see that it was a smaller scrap of the rich, black velvet. 'I only had to slowly pull these bits of velvet away from the props they were covering, and the objects seemed to materialise from nowhere.'

'Astounding,' muttered Barry.

'That's how frock-coat guy did Duckworth's.' Phyllis came and sat in the chair next to the Inspector's. 'Somehow he got involved with the company that was doing the window display for the Van Rockechild diamonds. He could've even just slipped in with the guys doing the job, and lurked about. He must've got hold of some extra dark blue velvet, the exact same material that was used for decking out the Duckworth's window. Maybe he just picked it up off the floor or somewhere while the setter-upperers were doing the display.'

The Inspector nodded and wondered how her turn of phrase would go down in a police report.

'It was triple velvet—it absorbs more light than any other sort. Then, when they were about to leave, he would have slipped on his dark blue velvet covering and gone and waited in a corner of the window, completely camouflaged against the curtain.'

'Invisible,' mused Barry.

'Uh-huh. And then later that night, he just went across to the stand, lifted the glass cube—we can't see that on the CCTV footage because the cube is so clean and spotless—and dropped a piece of the blue velvet onto the diamond necklace. And it'd disappeared! Then he picked up the swaddled jewels, put the cube back and returned to the corner.'

'What then?'

'Then, he just waited. Probably close to the door. He waited there all night, until the store opened again in the morning. When they discovered the jewels were gone, and as more people came into the display area and it got more crowded and everyone got excited, he would've just removed his velvet coverings and slipped away, with the necklace safely concealed on his person somewhere. It would've taken him only a few seconds to vamoose.'

The Chief Inspector ran his fingers over the black velvet in his lap. 'So, this felon has a knowledge of magic.'

'And not only that,' said Phyllis, her voice rising, 'he's following a pattern. He's going after a certain type of prize. Antiques or old things that are irreplaceable. I began wising up when I looked at what he's been after, and how he's been going about thieving them.'

'Hmmm. I'll get a check done. See if there's anyone on our books or recently released from prison who may have this sort of background. Some ex-magician with a criminal record . . .'

'Do you know of anyone like that?'

Barry shook his head. 'No. But now we've got more to go on. We've been scouring the city for him ever since the incident with the street—' He stopped himself. 'Well, we've been searching high and low. We can't find a trace of him.'

Phyllis's eyes narrowed and gleamed. 'Chief Inspector,' she said, 'I think I know where he's going to strike next!'

Purloining Picasso

'The Art Gallery?' Barry Inglis felt his blood become icy.

'The Picasso,' said Phyllis. 'He's going after rare works of art, Chief Inspector. The rarer and more valuable they are, the more attractive they are to him. That's his pattern. He's using magic to steal them. Magic that's all but been forgotten by most magicians working today.'

'Oh my giddy plexus,' said the Inspector. 'That's the last thing I need. The Picasso! *The Weeping* flipping *Walrus*. Heavens above, if that gets nicked, well . . . I'm back to writing parking tickets! That's the stuff of my nightmares, Miss Wong.'

Just then Harvey came into the cinema, followed closely by Daisy, who trotted down the aisle and sprang up onto Phyllis's lap.

'Phyll,' said her dad, 'you'd better come and see this. I think Clement must've sneaked some champagne. He's started doing funny voices and now he's entertaining us with a couple of spoons and some empty glasses and bottles and a fairly strange rendition of *The Flight of the Bumblebee* . . .'

'We'll be right there, Dad.'

'You'll kick yourselves if you miss it.' Harvey smiled and left them.

'I'll be facing a different kind of music if that painting gets stolen,' Barry said.

'When does it go on display?'

'Day after tomorrow. They're hanging it tomorrow afternoon. I'll be down there supervising the security, along with a few art experts and the curators.'

'I need to come with you.'

The Chief Inspector almost gave a small groan. 'I had a feeling you were going to say that.'

'I need to suss out the joint.'

'Miss Wong, do you know how hard it would be for me to justify having a young person like yourself at the location of my work? And the Metropolitan Art Gallery is hardly "the joint". No, it's—'

'—it's a public place,' said Phyllis, smiling.

'Er . . . yes, you're correct. It *is* a public place. But—'

'So, I'm a member of the public.'

'Yes, but the area where we'll be hanging the *Weeping Walrus* will be closed off tomorrow. It'll only be accessible to authorised people.'

Phyllis gave him her inscrutable smile. 'You can fix it, Chief Inspector. Trust me. If I'm right about this, you'll never have nightmares about writing parking tickets ever again.'

❃

The next day Phyllis found Chief Inspector Inglis leaning against a wall in a small alcove in the Metropolitan Art Gallery.

He was watching carefully as two men and two women in white coats unpacked the Picasso painting, wrapped in heavily padded linen, from a large wooden crate filled with straw. Several other men and women—some in police uniforms (including Constable Olofsson), others in plain clothes—stood by Barry, also carefully observing.

The Chief Inspector's face was expressionless; his blue eyes followed every movement of the packers, and his lips were fixed firmly in a straight line, which, to a casual observer, could have easily gone either way between a frown or a smile.

Because Phyllis knew him better than most, she could detect the small lines of concern that were knitting the upper edges of his eyebrows.

She went to the doorway of the alcove and whistled. If there had been a cab anywhere nearby, it would have stopped.

Everyone looked to the doorway.

The Chief Inspector didn't move, but slowly, almost imperceptibly, his eyes sleered to the left. He saw Phyllis standing there, smiling. He took a deep breath.

One of the uniformed police officers stepped up and told Phyllis that the small alcove gallery was off limits to the general public until tomorrow.

'That's swell,' said Phyllis. She looked across at the Inspector. 'He knows me.'

The police officer gave the Inspector a questioning glance.

The Inspector nodded.

The police officer let her in.

Phyllis greeted Constable Olofsson as she entered the narrow alcove gallery.

'Well, if it isn't the magician. Come to see your friend, have you?'

'I always come to the Gallery on my way home from school on Wednesdays,' Phyllis said. Which wasn't really true, but she didn't want to say too much if it meant trouble for the Chief Inspector.

'Look who's here,' Constable Olofsson said to Barry.

'Ah, Miss Wong.' Barry looked briefly at Phyllis before returning his gaze to the unpacking. 'What a pleasant surprise.'

The packers had laid the wrapped painting on the floor in front of the end wall of the small gallery. The wall had been painted a rich burgundy colour, especially for this hanging. The smell of fresh paint still hung in the air, and Phyllis wrinkled her nose at it.

The Chief Inspector gestured for his colleagues to assemble closer to the painting as it was being unwrapped. They all moved forward, leaving the Inspector and Phyllis by the opposite wall. Phyllis dumped her schoolbag on the floor.

'So it's in there?' she asked.

'That is what we're presuming,' he answered.

'And that's where they're displaying it?'

He nodded. 'Right in the centre of the wall. It'll be the only painting in this smaller space. The Gallery decided to exhibit it in here because they thought it'd be safer in a contained area. Less likelihood of a thief being able to make off with it. They thought.'

'They don't know frock-coat guy.'

Barry's eyebrows knitted some more.

The last ropes had been untied, and the packers slowly peeled away the padded linen. Two of them lifted one end of the painting and, carefully, all four of them slid the painting across the floor on its mat of padded linen and rested it against the burgundy wall.

The packers, the police and the curators stepped back to view it.

'Come on,' said Barry. He took Phyllis closer, and they also had a good look.

The painting was large and sat in a wide gold frame that had small scrollwork carved into it. The walrus's colours were bright, bold, daring, and Phyllis liked the way its green and mauve splashes seemed to hint at a deep thoughtfulness in the creature, a thoughtfulness verging on sadness.

'A hundred and twenty million, eh?' said the police officer who had met Phyllis at the door.

'To the right person,' said Constable Olofsson.

'I won't be buying many of *them*. Not on our salary,' said another officer.

One of the curators sniffed loudly and gave them a withering look.

Chief Inspector Inglis and Phyllis watched as the curators began fiddling with the hanging wires on the wall.

'He's going to try to take it out of the frame,' Phyllis said quietly.

'What makes you think so?'

'He only takes things he can carry without attracting attention. Smallish things. He's working alone. The blue wren fitted into his bag, the diamond necklace into his pocket.' Phyllis watched as the curators started inspecting the back of the *Weeping Walrus*. 'He's going to cut the painting out of the frame, roll it up and fold it, and take it out in his coat.'

Barry spoke just as quietly. 'We'll have officers here from this moment onwards. At no time will this gallery be unattended. We will also have undercover officers at all the entrances and exits. He won't be able to get within sneezing distance.'

'They don't know his magic. You need to attach some sort of tracking device to the painting. Not on the frame, but on the canvas.'

The Chief Inspector listened.

'That way, if he *does* get it, you can follow him. You can have a chance, at least.'

The Chief Inspector nodded. 'You think in ways that I find extraordinary, Miss Wong. Excuse me.'

He took out his phone and made a call.

Half an hour later, two people from Surveillance arrived at the Metropolitan Art Gallery. An hour after that, the *Weeping Walrus* had a tiny, undetectable addition impregnated seamlessly into the outer edge of the canvas.

Phyllis had watched the whole procedure with keen interest.

Then the painting had finally been hung and positioned and straightened and lit and fussed over. It looked vibrant against the burgundy wall; so bright that it could have been painted yesterday rather than all those decades ago.

Everyone moved out of the gallery and mingled in their own small groups for a few minutes outside the doorway.

'You should be getting home,' the Chief Inspector said to Phyllis as the people started to leave. 'Your father will be worried. And Daisy needs her walk.'

'Yep,' Phyllis said. Darkness would soon be falling outside.

'I'll get Constable Olofsson to run you back.' Barry turned to her. 'And, Miss Wong? Would you like to attend the opening tomorrow night? As my guest for the big unveiling? Like I said, it'll be a great night for the horse doovers. You can bring your friend if you'd like; the xylophonist.'

Phyllis grinned. 'Why not?' She thought it would be fun for her and Clem to watch all the people dressed up to the nines and to eavesdrop on their conversations. And it would be an extra celebration for Clem, who was having his plaster removed tomorrow morning.

'Good,' said the Inspector. 'That would be a fine thing, Miss Wong. A fine thing, indeed.'

The Gallery was getting ready to close, and cleaners in white coats were beginning to come through the deserted areas, sweeping up and polishing the bronze and marble sculptures here and there. Barry arranged for Constable Olofsson to escort Phyllis home in one of the cars. Then he briefed two of the uniformed men and they positioned themselves at the doorway to the small alcove gallery.

It was going to be a long night for them. And an even longer one for Chief Inspector Barry Inglis.

❃

'Man, I didn't know we had to dress up!'

'You look fine, Clem. Even with that chocolate milkshake stain all over your shirt.'

Clement and Phyllis were weaving through all the zhooshed-up adults in the main foyer of the Metropolitan Art Gallery. Waiters and waitresses bearing silver trays of canapés and appetisers and tall flutes of champagne waltzed through the crowd, and more than once a waiter almost tripped over Clement, who had an unfailing knack of being able to get in people's way.

'Oh, look at that, Phyll!' Clement had stopped by a pedestal that had a small, nude, greenish bronze sculpture of a Balinese woman whose limbs were entwined all about herself on it, and he was blushing. He whipped out his phone and took a photo of her.

Phyllis rolled her eyes.

She felt her shoulder bag starting to wriggle against her side. 'Clem, come with me!'

She grabbed him by the wrist and led him through the crowd to a less populated corner of the foyer. There, she stood between Clement and the wall, slid her bag halfway off her shoulder and opened the top. Out popped Daisy's small snout, and the little dog blinked her brown eyes at the sudden onslaught of bright light.

'Hey!' said Clement, patting her between her ears. 'Why'd you bring the Deebs?'

'She was really clingy,' answered Phyllis. 'She doesn't often get that way, but she was tonight. She doesn't want to be left alone when she's like this.'

'I'll get her one of those little bits of chicken those waiters are handing out. Stay here, okay?'

Before she could say anything, Clement was off, hobbling a little and narrowly avoiding colliding into a pedestal upon which rested a marble bust by Bernini of a startled-looking, curly-bearded gentleman.

Phyllis shook her head. She turned so her back was to the foyer. Gently she stroked Daisy's snout. Daisy gave her fingers a quick lick. 'Everything's fine,' Phyllis told her, smiling.

Daisy blinked trustingly. Then she gave a little gargle and her head disappeared back into the comfort of the shoulder bag.

'I'm surprised you got that past security,' came a firm but friendly voice from behind her.

'Hello, Chief Inspector,' Phyllis said, quickly folding the flap over the top of the bag. She turned, and her eyes widened. 'Well, someone's dolled up!'

'My gala attire,' Barry said, smoothing down the lapels of his dark blue pinstripe suit. 'I'm glad you came.'

'I'm glad you asked me.'

Clement came bustling back, his hands full of chicken portions and napkins and some other things that looked like fishcakes with a pale orange condiment dribbling off them. 'Hey, look at all this—oh, hi, Chief Inspector.'

'Evening, Clement. You won't be getting stuck into the champagne again tonight, will you?'

'Um . . . no, sir.' He offered some of his bounty to Phyllis and Barry.

They both politely declined, so he started

stuffing the tidbits into his mouth as he watched all the elegant people milling about.

The Inspector looked out across the foyer. Keeping his eyes on the scene before him, he said to Phyllis: 'Care for a sneak preview? They've adjusted the lighting on the painting. It looks even more impressive than yesterday. Matter of fact, I wouldn't have known it was the same painting when I saw it an hour ago.'

A tremor of something went up Phyllis's spine when she heard that. 'Sure. Lead the way,' she said.

Barry took her through the crowd, with Clement scurrying along behind, grabbing food from unsuspecting waiters along the way.

They came to the entrance to the alcove gallery and the Inspector nodded to the two police officers on duty. One of them removed an end of a plush red silken rope from a smart brass bollard, and the Inspector, Phyllis, Clement (and Daisy) went into the gallery. The officer repositioned the red rope and went back to looking supremely bored.

'In half an hour, all that lot out there will be swarming in here to see the *Weeping Walrus*,' Barry Inglis said. 'For the first time in decades, it'll be on public view again.'

'No it won't,' Phyllis said, her voice low, her heart beating fast as she looked at the painting on the wall. 'That's not the Picasso. He's already taken it!'

Disturbing the universe

A small roped barrier had been erected in front of the *Weeping Walrus* to prevent people from getting too close. Phyllis put her bag gently down and stepped over the rope.

Her bag gave a little wriggle, then was still.

'Look,' she said to Chief Inspector Inglis and Clement. 'It's not real.' She raised her palm, spread her long fingers and gave the *Weeping Walrus* a hard slap, right in the centre of its lopsided face.

The Inspector gasped and his hand shot to his mouth.

The painting and the burgundy wall behind it rippled like a curtain billowing in a strong breeze.

'See?' said Phyllis. 'This is a painted backdrop. It's just a small section of the wall behind it, made to look like the Picasso is still hanging here.' She stepped back, being careful not to fall over the rope barrier, and scrutinised the wall from ceiling to floor. 'He's clever. He only replicated a small section of the wall—just a little wider than the painting itself. Now . . . where're the edges . . . ?'

She stretched her arms wide and ran them across the backdrop. Her fingers curled around the almost-invisible edges where the backdrop blended against the real wall, about half a metre behind it. 'Got it.' She grabbed hold of the edges and gave a sharp yank downwards.

The backdrop popped out of the hooks which attached it to the ceiling and plummeted to the floor. Phyllis stepped out of the way just in time.

The Chief Inspector's face crumpled. There on the wall hung the empty golden scrolled frame, with the *Weeping Walrus* nowhere to be seen. 'Oh, good lord! Just like you said. He's cut it out!'

'Man,' said Clement, reaching into his pocket for his phone. 'This is *baaaaaaad*.'

'No photos, Clement,' said Barry. 'And no calls.'

Clement shrugged. 'You're the boss.' He quickly pocketed the phone again.

The Chief Inspector pulled out a small earpiece-microphone from his breast pocket and spoke into it. Then he went to the two officers at the doorway and told them to keep people away, using any deterrent they had to. Fortunately, the wall displaying the empty frame was around a corner from the doorway, so a clear view into the alcove gallery was not possible from the foyer.

'Why aren't we tracking it?' asked Phyllis impatiently. 'You put the device into it yesterday. Why aren't you—?'

Barry raised his hand to silence her, as his eyes moved slowly across the empty gold frame. 'What I can't fathom,' he said, 'is how he got in here to nab it. We've had people watching the whole time, ever since they unpacked the confounded thing yesterday. It's as if he's a—'

'Yes, Chief?' said Constable Olofsson, appearing from around the corner. She took one look at the wall and said, '*Järnspikar*!'

Clement smirked—even though he spoke no Swedish, he could tell that the word wasn't one you'd hear in the classroom.

'Yes, Constable, it is far from ideal. Have you got the tracker?' asked the Chief Inspector.

Constable Olofsson took a small leather case that was hanging by a strap from her shoulder. She flipped open the cover and pressed a button on the console inside.

The Inspector, Phyllis and Clement gathered around to watch the screen on the console come to life.

Phyllis's bag gave a small growl in the corner. Phyllis picked it up, patted the side of it, put it over her shoulder and came back to watch the screen.

A pattern of streets emerged, an aerial view of crisscrossing yellow lines interspersed with patches of green. Phyllis assumed the green bits were parks or garden areas of the city.

'Nothing downtown,' said Constable Olofsson after a few moments.

'Go east,' the Inspector told her.

She swiped her finger across the screen, and the grid pattern slid to the left. Now more streets appeared, and fewer and fewer patches of green.

'This is near the harbour,' Constable Olofsson said. 'Not yet at the water, but getting close.'

'What're you looking for?' asked Phyllis.

'A flashing light, Phyll,' said Clement, in an I-know-all-about-these-things-because-I'm-into-all-the-latest-technology sort of voice.

'A *pulsating* light,' Constable Olofsson corrected him. 'This is the latest model. No *flashing* any more.'

Clement looked impressed.

'Nothing,' said Barry, frowning as the screen lit up his face. 'Okay, next stop, the old warehouse district. North, by the disused wharves.'

The constable swiped again. A new district appeared. Phyllis saw fewer streets, and no green areas at all. Instead, there were many large patches of dark brown.

'Dismal,' Phyllis said to herself. And then she had an instinct. 'He'll be in that area. Somewhere.'

The Chief Inspector's eyes moved around the screen, waiting, watching . . .

Suddenly, a small red dot appeared. It grew brighter, and faded, then grew bright again and faded. And so it continued.

'Gotcha!' muttered the Inspector through clenched teeth.

Constable Olofsson said, 'It's not moving. It's stationary.'

'Makes it even better for us,' said Barry. 'He's settled. I hate chases. They play havoc with my stomach. Okay, listen carefully, Constable. This has to be a quiet operation. The boys at the door here are keeping people away. We'll slip out, undetected. Just you and me. And my little friend here.' He patted the left-hand side of his pinstriped coat.

For a moment, Phyllis thought he meant her; then she realised that he had a gun. She listened to him carefully—she'd never seen him in full police mode like this before.

'You drive,' Barry said to Constable Olofsson. 'No sirens, just nice and steady, like a big old cat creeping through the jungle.'

Constable Olofsson gave him a strange look.

'I want this boy brought down,' said the Chief Inspector. 'I want him sent away. I want to see him dancing in that pale moonlight . . .'

Constable Olofsson gave him another strange look.

He cleared his throat and lowered his voice a little. 'Okay, let's go. Let's get out of here.' He started for the doorway.

'I'm coming, too!' Phyllis said.

Barry stopped and turned. 'What?'

'I'm coming. This is my case too. I know everything that's happened. I got us here.'

It was as if a switch had been flicked; the Inspector's manner changed instantly and he pulled his I've-just-eaten-a-sour-lemon face. 'Miss Wong, I can't allow you to—'

'If she's going, so am I!' blurted Clement. 'We work as a team!'

Now Phyllis gave Clement a strange look.

'Hey, who rolled you out of the way of that machine?' asked Clement. 'Who took the breaks for you, Phyllis Wong?'

'Look,' said Barry, 'I can't allow you both to

come with us. This could be very dangerous. It's no place for—' And there he stopped, for Phyllis Wong was giving him a look; a look of determination, of calm, strong resolve. A look which Barry knew was saying to him that if he *didn't* let her come along, then their friendship would never be the same again.

He put his fingers to his temples. 'Oh, all right. We've wasted enough time here already. You can come.'

'Chief Inspector?' queried Constable Olofsson. 'Are you sure?'

'Both of us?' asked Clement.

'He has to come too,' Phyllis said to Barry. She flashed Clement a grin.

Barry took his hands down and waved them in front of him, defeated. 'Yeah. Okay. The both of you. But you must, I repeat *must*, stay out of the way.'

He gave Phyllis a stern look. She still had that determined expression, but now she was also smiling at him.

❀

'Turn right into Vargren Street.'

Constable Olofsson was a good driver, but despite Barry's advice to remain calm, she couldn't resist taking some of the corners in such a way that there was a slight squeal of rubber. This delighted Clement, and made Daisy wriggle-acious, causing her to pop her head out of Phyllis's bag. Phyllis had to pat her quickly and pop her back inside.

Now they were turning into a long, dirty street, the sort of street that many decades ago would have been bustling, but which nowadays was mainly deserted, day and night, as were many of the disused warehouses and factories that stood like broken, blackened teeth against the dark mouth of the harbour.

The Chief Inspector had been watching the tracking screen as they had been travelling. As they'd come closer to their destination, the small red dot had been pulsating brighter and faster.

'Are we there yet?' asked Clement.

Barry shot him a warning glance. Clement wouldn't ask again.

They drove past piles of garbage bags lining the sidewalk. Phyllis saw a swarm of rats inveigling itself into one of the opened bags. She shuddered.

'That's it up ahead,' Barry said quietly. 'The old warehouse with the glass-block windows and the two headless lion statues on the steps.'

Phyllis peered through the car window. The tall narrow windows in the front of the three-storey warehouse were so grimy that they showed no reflection of the almost-full moon.

'Pull up here,' Barry said. 'We'll walk and surprise him.'

Constable Olofsson brought the car to a smooth, silent stop.

Barry turned to Phyllis and Clement. 'You two'll have to stay here. It's the way it has to be. I'm sorry.'

Constable Olofsson spoke up. 'We can't leave them in the car, Chief. Not in a neighbourhood like this.'

'Yes, Chief Inspector,' said Phyllis. 'Anything might happen.'

'Yeah,' said Clement. 'It could be nasty.'

'Oh, heavens above.' Barry shook his head. 'They'll have my badge if I—'

Phyllis gave him that look again.

He sighed and opened his door to get out. 'Okay then, you're coming with us! But you both stay behind me and the Constable at all times. And I mean *all* times. Understood?'

'Understood,' said Phyllis, getting out from the back and slinging Daisy's bag over her shoulder.

'*Comprendo*,' said Clement, getting out the other side.

'Now, quietly,' said Barry.

Phyllis and Clement followed the Chief Inspector and Constable Olofsson along the dingy sidewalk and up to the headless lions. Daisy squirmed a little in the bag, but Phyllis settled her with a few gentle pats.

Barry had a final look at the tracking screen. The red dot was pulsating so strongly it seemed fit to burst through the glass of the screen. He nodded at Constable Olofsson, turned off the screen and gave it to her. She put it back into her leather case and slipped the strap across her shoulders.

Barry went up the four steps to the weather-beaten doors. Old flakes of dark green paint were dotted across the wood. He placed his hand against one of the doors and gave a gentle push.

Locked.

He took out a pencil-thin flashlight from his coat pocket. Constable Olofsson took out an identical one from a pocket in her trousers.

The Chief Inspector pointed his light at the old brass lock. His eyebrows gathered in the centre as he took from his pocket a small cylindrical brass implement. He slid the top off it, rotated the round end, and out emerged a small skeleton key. This he put into the lock and gave it a small, quiet jiggle.

The door swung silently open.

Phyllis's heart beat faster. She had a feeling,

somewhere deep down inside her, that she was about to enter a place that might change her life; that might alter the course of all her days ahead. Sometimes revelations can lead to the most unexpected places . . .

The Inspector and Constable Olofsson entered the building, Phyllis and Clement bringing up the rear.

The ground floor was a large, open area, empty except for a long wooden bench that ran diagonally down the middle of the space. The bench was littered with old paint cans, newspapers and a few empty wooden boxes. The flashlight beams passed across them, picking out a fine curtain of cobwebs hanging between the boxes and cans.

Barry withdrew his gun. He lowered his arm and held it by his side, slightly out from his leg, the barrel of the pistol pointing towards the floorboards.

Treading lightly, he moved around behind the bench and swept his flashlight beam across it. He looked across to Constable Olofsson and shook his head. Then he came back to the stairs that led up to the next two storeys.

Clement pushed his glasses to the top of his nose. He was breathing heavily, the air making small whistling sounds in and out of his nostrils.

Barry gestured with his head to the others and they began climbing the stairs after him.

The stairs were old and wooden, and the balustrade had fallen away halfway between the ground floor and second storey. 'Stay close to the wall and step lightly,' the Inspector whispered. 'These stairs'll probably be creaksville.'

If she hadn't been so shaky, Phyllis would've almost giggled.

Up they climbed to the second-floor landing. Barry and the constable swept their lights across the space on their right. This floor was totally empty. A thick carpet of dust caked the floor. The tall glass-block windows were gloomy and dreary, and many of the square panes had cracks running through them.

Phyllis looked up the stairs. Her heartbeat was thumping like drums in the jungle.

Barry waved his hand at them and began climbing the stairs. Slowly, in single file, they followed.

Clement, walking behind Phyllis (and Daisy), went slowly; his newly healed leg was not yet able to take stairs at normal pace.

They came to the landing on the third floor. Through a doorway was another room. Unlike the others they had seen, this one seemed to be in use.

Barry gestured for them to follow him, and in they went. Along the wall to the left was a long table covered by a wide black cloth. There was another long table at the far end of the room, next to a tall, arched window. This window was different from the others below; it was not comprised of glass blocks, but smaller, older-looking panes of hexagonal glass, lead-lined around the edges.

There was an antique chaise longue upholstered in olive green silk in the far right corner. A few suitcases with old travel stickers were stacked near this, and there was a coatstand with several overcoats and hats on it.

Phyllis gasped as Constable Olofsson's light travelled across the coatstand. 'Look! The frock coat!'

'Is that his?' asked the Chief Inspector.

'That's his,' Phyllis said. 'That's his.'

'Where is the little toad?' the Inspector said, moving his beam around the room.

Phyllis put down Daisy's bag and turned to the table behind her. She pulled back the long black cloth. 'Chief!' she whispered. 'Look!'

Barry turned, as did Constable Olofsson, and they illuminated the objects on the table. There lay the blue wren bookend, sitting next to the tall black bag that frock-coat guy had always turned up with at Mrs Lowerblast's. Next to this, arranged on a velvet jewellery display, was the Van Rockechild necklace, its diamonds sparkling brilliantly in the flashlight beams. And, at the far end of the table, half-unrolled, was Picasso's *Weeping Walrus*.

Phyllis got the feeling that the stolen goods had been only recently laid out, ready to be packed away. Possibly, she thought, for a trip that was about to be taken.

'Man!' said Clement. 'This is better than *Zombie Accountants from Boomdiddy Vostock*!'

'Bullseye,' muttered Barry.

Phyllis turned the black bag around. Sure enough, it was cut away at the rear. She put her hand in and moved the elevator-flap up and down.

'You're brilliant, Miss Wong,' the Chief Inspector said. 'Brilliant and astonishing.'

'*As if you'd know the virtues of those particular qualities*,' came a deep, rasping voice from behind them.

They spun around to see a tall, slender man standing by the chaise longue. He was wearing a white shirt, powder-blue waistcoat and slim-cut, dark blue trousers. Around his neck was tied a crimson and green cravat. His longish dark hair was swept back from his high forehead and hung down to his shoulders. Constable Olofsson's light picked out a scar running from his eye to a place halfway down his cheek, and he sported a large, black-framed monocle in his right eye. This was attached to his waistcoat's upper pocket by a thin ribbon of black velvet.

The Inspector moved his pistol out of sight, behind his leg. 'Who are you?' he asked.

'I am un-*touch*-able,' the man said. He spoke *at* them, not *to* them.

'You're under arrest, that's what you are,' said Barry Inglis.

The man took a step closer to them. 'HA!' he snapped. He removed his monocle, opened his eyes maniacally wide, and stared at them, long and silent.

And he froze like that.

Phyllis was the first to notice that his eyes almost *glowed* bright green!

'Man,' Clement whispered to her. 'This guy's freaking me out!'

The man continued to stare at them without saying a word or moving a muscle. Even the Chief Inspector, who had seen some strange things during his time in the force, was unnerved by the weirdness of the man's stance and manner.

The only sign of life in the man was in his eyes, as they glowed brighter, then subsided, then glowed again.

Phyllis thought the man seemed to not be there, yet he *was* there. It was as if he were wafting in and out of their presence . . . like an image suspended in time, or a character in a film where the projector has stalled and frozen him stock-still.

Then, slowly, the man's mouth opened and he blinked. He spoke again. 'You . . . you . . . you . . . you . . . are in-con-veniencing me.' His voice rose at the end of his sentence, but still remained deep and haughty.

'Inconvenience? You ain't seen inconvenience yet,' the Inspector said. 'You haven't even dreamt of it . . .'

The man put his monocle back in. Slowly his head turned, and his green gaze settled on Phyllis. His eyes glowed brighter. 'Aaaaah. *You*. I thought I'd finished you. I thought I'd sent you to your kingdom . . . your kingdom . . . your kingdom come!'

Phyllis stared at him. An image crossed her mind; an image she had seen in the basement amongst Wallace Wong's props and illusions. Slowly she pointed to the table behind her. 'How do you come to know about this magic?' she asked.

'Magic?' he sneered. 'Magic? What would you know . . . know . . . know . . . about *magic*?' He spat the word from his lips as if it were poison.

'I know how you pulled off the crimes,' said Phyllis calmly. 'How you got the blue wren bookend there.'

'That's mine. Always has . . . has . . . has been.'

'Liar! You stole that from Mrs Lowerblast!'

'You silly . . . silly . . . silly *girl*. What makes you think that that bookend is the only one of its kind? There are more in the worlds than you realise . . .'

Barry's grip on his pistol tightened.

Phyllis held up the black bag. 'Here's the proof you stole it from her. You used an old effect, one that people have all but forgotten today!'

'HA!' spat the green-eyed man, his eyes pulsating at her.

'And you used black art to get the Van Rockechild diamonds,' Phyllis said. 'Yes, you did! You used old magic!'

'You stupid . . . stupid . . . stupid . . .'

'Watch that mouth of yours, sunshine!' warned Barry.

'You think that those tricks are *magic*?' spat the man. 'What foolishness. No, you idiots, I have found *real* magic . . . real . . . real . . . *real* . . . I have found something far beyond the trickery and the gimmickry and the false-bottomed boxes . . . Those little pieces of illusions which I utilised to obtain those few valuables are *nothing* compared to what I do! To what I *know*!'

'You're mad!' the Inspector said. 'You think you'll be able to move these on? They're all traceable. You try to sell the Picasso or the Van Rockechild diamonds or the blue wren—there's nowhere in this world they'll not be traced!'

At this, the man raised his hands, claw-like, and held them at shoulder-height for a few frozen moments. Then he blinked and his eyes grew brighter, greener, as though a surge of colour had been injected into them. 'Oh,' he said, 'I know a place where they will not be traced. A place where they will be worth a hundred times what they're worth here!'

'In your dreams,' said Constable Olofsson.

'Ah, dreams *are* a world, yes, yes, yes,' said the man. 'But they are not not not not the world of which I speak! You fools! Has it ever occurred to you why I have been taking things that are small . . . that are easily *transportable*? You pathetic inhabitants of your own little lives, of your own little worlds, with your narrow ways of thought, and your here-and-now, mind-locked ideas! Look beyond, beyond, *beyond*!'

Barry shook his head. 'Cut the attitude,' he said. 'There's one thing I don't understand . . .'

'Only one thing?' asked the man, his voice full of ridicule. 'What might that be, sir?'

The Chief ignored the sarcasm. 'We know how you stole the bookend. We know how you did the Duckworth's window, how you slunk in there with the display fitters and then hung around afterwards. We know how you got the Picasso. Just tell me this: how did you get *into* the Art Gallery to put up the backdrop and grab the painting? We had people there around the clock. There was no time . . .'

Phyllis Wong's eyes narrowed. 'I know how he did it,' she said slowly. 'He travelled there.'

The man looked at her, and a strange flicker crossed his face, as though he had just recognised something he hadn't seen before.

Phyllis smiled at him. 'He *found* the time . . .'

Barry looked at her.

'Oh, yes,' said the man. 'Oh, yes, little girl, I found the time. I *always* find the time. I saw the set-up at the Gallery. I saw the colour of the wall. I saw the painting from the inter . . . the inter . . . the *internet.* I replicated it, on a backdrop—the wall and the painting, with all the correct shadows and features of reality. Then I went back, back to the

Gallery and back to the day before, after the painting had been unpacked. There was a window of time where everyone came out of the small gallery after the painting was finally hung. I slipped in, in a white coat, similar to those of the cleaners'. I knew their uniform. I got in there. I can get . . . get . . . get . . . into places others can't. I quickly hung the backdrop, cut out the painting and returned.'

'What?' said Constable Olofsson.

'What?' said Clement.

The man looked carefully at Phyllis. 'When you *smiled* . . . you are related to him, aren't you?'

Phyllis didn't answer.

'Wallace Wong!' spat the man. 'You are related to him, are you NOT?'

'I am,' said Phyllis.

The man's voice became louder. 'Ah. Ah. Ah. Ah. AH! You know, there was a backdrop once. A backdrop I painted for him. I am the greatest backdrop artist of my time. Of all time. Of all time to come. It was New York harbour.'

'1926,' said Phyllis, nodding.

'Yes,' said the man. 'You have seen it?'

'I have.'

'Did you notice the signature in the corner?'

'I did, Mr Okyto.'

The man's eyes glowed greener.

'So that's who you are,' said the Chief Inspector. 'Okyto. You don't look Japanese.'

'That's because I am not. It is a name I took for my profession.'

Constable Olofsson spoke up: 'What're you trying to pull? If you'd painted that backdrop, you'd be over 120 years old!'

The man went totally still for ten seconds, and the green in his eyes became more vivid. Then he took a breath and said, 'What makes you think I'm *not*?'

'He travels through time,' said Phyllis Wong.

'What?' said the Inspector, looking at her again.

The man pointed a finger at Phyllis and began shouting: 'You meddling little . . . little . . . little . . .'

Daisy's head appeared out of the top of Phyllis's bag. The little dog heard the angry words and saw the green-eyed man directing them at Phyllis. Then she saw him take a step towards her.

Daisy leapt from the bag and pelted towards Okyto. In two seconds she had her teeth buried in one of his ankles.

The man shrieked, kicking his leg hard into the air. Daisy flew off his ankle and sailed across the room. She landed with an awful thud on the floor, sliding across it and slamming into the wall. She lay there, still.

'No!' Phyllis rushed to her, past Okyto, but he lashed out and grabbed her. He hoisted her in front of him and, in an instant, he reached around to the table behind him and swiped up a long knife. The blade glinted in the glow from the flashlights.

'I'm going away,' he said, almost snarling the words. 'And I'm going to take the meddlesome one with me! Maybe she will get to meet her great-grandfather!'

Daisy gave a tiny whimper in the corner.

'Let her go!' ordered Barry Inglis. 'She's done you no harm!'

'Oh, the world . . . the world . . . the *world* . . . is *always* doing me harm. Always.' He raised the blade to Phyllis's throat. 'Let us disturb the universe somewhere else! There are other treasures to be GOT!'

'Please,' Phyllis whispered. 'Let me—'

'Oh, you're coming with ME!' he snarled.

'That's what you think, sweetheart!' Inspector Inglis shouted at him.

There was a sudden *whoosh*ing sound, and a small hard bit of cardboard hurtled through the air like a spear. It hit Okyto's monocle, shattering the glass and making it fly out in all directions.

'*Aaaarrrggggghhhhhhh*!' the man screamed, letting go of Phyllis and bringing his hands to his eye. 'Noooo, my eye, *noooooo*!' A trickle of blood appeared between his fingers.

Phyllis ran to Daisy and scooped up the little dog. Daisy shook her head and licked Phyllis's hands.

The Inspector and Constable Olofsson approached Okyto. He flailed one arm, trying to keep them away. He moved backwards and bumped into the chaise longue and the coatstand, sending it crashing to the ground. He turned and, half-blinded, he slashed the air with the knife.

Constable Olofsson jumped back, the blade missing her by millimetres.

Clement took Phyllis and Daisy and hurried them out of the way to the landing.

The Chief Inspector circled Okyto, his pistol ready.

Okyto slashed the air again, and Barry pulled himself back. Then he lunged at Okyto, and Okyto stumbled, slashing at the Inspector. Barry pulled back, circling Okyto. He lunged at Okyto again, and again Okyto stumbled—this time backwards, his feet getting tangled in the sleeves of his frock coat on the floor. He spun around, trying to slash at Barry Inglis with his knife . . .

. . . and then, the singularities of Mr Okyto's time—of the time here, of the time now—pushed against his balance, and the forces of his existence juddered mightily. He fell, backwards, fast, straight through the window behind him.

There was an ear-splitting crash of glass, followed by a muffled scream. And then a hollow, heavy sound three storeys below.

Phyllis was scarcely breathing as Daisy licked her fingers.

'It's okay,' said Constable Olofsson. 'He's gone now.'

'That he is,' said the Chief Inspector, peering down through the shattered window. He frowned. 'That he is.'

Clear

Later, after the forensic pathologists and all the other police experts had been to inspect the scene, and after the valuables had been safely transported back to police headquarters and Constable Olofsson had taken Clement home, Chief Inspector Inglis drove Phyllis and Daisy back to the Wallace Wong Building.

It was a cold, clear night; a light frost had settled on the lower grassy verges by the sidewalks. As Phyllis looked out the window of the squad car, the frost seemed to be telling her that things had settled.

After a while, the Inspector broke the silence. 'Are you all right?'

Phyllis smiled. 'Oh, I'm swell, thank you. Daisy's swell too.'

'Good.'

'Are you all right?'

'Hmm. I believe I, also, am swell.'

'Good.'

'You know, I have already made this observation, Miss Wong, but I'll make it again, as a good thing is always worth repeating: you are brilliant and astonishing.'

'Thank you.' Phyllis blushed.

'No, thank *you*. Without you, things would've turned out very differently.'

On Phyllis's lap, Daisy was busy licking her dainty paws. She was glad to be going home.

'Chief Inspector?'

'How may I be of assistance?' he asked, his eyes on the street ahead.

'Where did you learn to shoot a card like that?'

'Oh, you learn all sorts of things at Detective School. We used to shoot cards into a hat in our spare time. I became very adept at it. Won the stakes every time, as a matter of fact.' His eyes twinkled. 'You're not the only one with a trick up your sleeve, you know.'

'Ha. Chief Inspector?'

'Yes?'

'I've got another question.'

'Proceed, Miss Wong.'

'How come you never smile?'

'Don't I?'

'I've never seen you. Sometimes it looks like you're about to, but you never do it.'

'Ah. Well. Maybe I'm saving all that for my old age.'

'Ha! You'll never get old, Inspector Inglis.'

'Not when I've got you around, I won't.'

'Hey, we're almost home. Put the siren on! Please? Please?'

The Inspector sighed. 'Oh, come on, you know we can't—'

'Go on. I dare you.'

Barry sighed again.

It was no use.

He could never argue with her.

He gave in to defeat like a true gentleman.

On that frosty, clear night, the last few minutes of their journey home became a blaring cacophony of noise that woke up much of the quiet, still neighbourhood of Phyllis Wong.

The nine of diamonds

EXTRACTED FROM THE OFFICIAL REPORT OF CHIEF INSPECTOR BARRY W. INGLIS, FINE ARTS AND ANTIQUES SQUAD, REGARDING THE OKYTO INCIDENT:

I must admit that there are still some baffling questions that remain unanswered regarding the case of the Okyto thefts. These are but a few:

We still don't have the full identity of the perpetrator; the man who called himself Okyto. He made several bizarre claims on the night of his near apprehension, the most peculiar being that he was able to travel through time. In my opinion, this was nothing more than the rantings of a deranged and dangerous man.

I believe he had some sort of mental condition; he frequently went into what can only be described as minor catatonic states, when he would freeze for extended periods, and a strange green glow would fill his eyes—not just the pupils, but the whites as well. This could have been one of the symptoms of some physical aberration, or some mental peculiarity. He also repeated words, often three or four times in mid-sentence. It is my opinion that his brain was clearly not functioning well at all.

One other strange thing: our researchers, upon trying to ascertain the perpetrator's identity, found a man named Okyto who was a scenic artist and theatrical designer. (The perpetrator claimed to be a backdrop painter, the finest of his day.) But, according to newspaper sources of the time, this man named Okyto was actively working in 1832. The last trace we have found of him was in 1897. These references are the only records we have discovered of a man with that name and that background.

The most strange thing about the whole incident, however, is this: when I looked through the broken window, I saw the body of the perpetrator lying in a position which clearly indicated that he was no more. Later, when the forensic pathologists arrived, the body was gone. We searched the nearby vicinity, but no trace was found of it. Nor was there any trail of blood leading from the scene. It was as if he had vanished without a trace.

All of the stolen property has been returned to its rightful owners. As we do not have custody of the perpetrator, the case will not go to court. This is a relief to me, as I had given my word to a colleague that certain facts would remain confidential and would not be divulged to anyone else. Now, with no court case looming, I do not have to break my promise.

One final point to note: the weapon I used to throw the perpetrator off guard was a small playing card. It is one that I always carry around in my breast pocket. I have found, in my experience, that sometimes when you think beyond the seemingly normal, the smallest things you have can alter events and change the course of happenings in the most unexpected of ways.

(signed)
Barry Inglis
Chief Inspector
Fine Arts and Antiques Squad

The author

Find out more about Phyllis Wong at

www.phylliswong.com